MARVEL CINEMATIC UNIVERSE
PHASE ONE

MARVEL

CAPTAIN AMERICA
THE FIRST AVENGER

MARVEL CINEMATIC UNIVERSE
PHASE ONE

MARVEL

CAPTAIN AMERICA
THE FIRST AVENGER

WITHDRAWN

Adapted by ALEX IRVINE

Based on the Screenplay by
CHRISTOPHER MARKUS & STEPHEN McFEELY

Produced by KEVIN FEIGE

Directed by JOE JOHNSTON

(L)(B)
LITTLE, BROWN AND COMPANY
New York   Boston

marvelkids.com

© 2014 MARVEL

Little, Brown and Company

Hachette Book Group
1290 Avenue of the Americas, New York, NY 10104
Visit us at lb-kids.com

Little, Brown and Company is a division of Hachette Book Group, Inc.
The Little, Brown name and logo are trademarks of Hachette Book Group, Inc.

The publisher is not responsible for websites (or their content) that are not owned by the publisher.

First Edition: November 2014

Library of Congress Cataloging-in-Publication Data
Irvine, Alexander (Alexander C.)
   Phase one, Captain America / adapted by Alex Irvine.—First edition.
     pages cm.—(Marvel cinematic universe)
   ISBN 978-0-316-25632-2 (hardcover)
   1. Graphic novels. I. Captain America, the first avenger
(Motion picture) II. Title.
   PZ7.I673Phc 2014
   741.5'973—dc23

                                                              2014027635

10 9 8 7 6

RRD-C

Printed in the United States of America

CHAPTER 1

Steve Rogers stood nervously in line at the recruitment center in Bayonne, New Jersey. Ahead of him, men stepped up one by one. And one by one, they got approved to join the army. Steve sighed and waited for his turn, which seemed as if it would never come. Looking around, he noticed several newspaper headlines about a brutal attack on a small Norwegian town that had left civilians hurt and homeless.

America was at war. Across the ocean, Europe was

full of gunfire and explosions. Men, women, and children were losing their lives and their homes as enemy forces invaded country after country. It had been going on for two years before America got involved, but then Pearl Harbor had happened. Now soldiers from the United States were flooding Europe, hoping to help the good guys win. But it wasn't going to be an easy—or a short—fight.

Steve felt the now-familiar rush of anger—and frustration. He wanted to be over there fighting more than anything in the world. But try as he might, he couldn't get past anyone in the recruitment centers, no matter how many attempts he made.

Steve had never been a big guy. Growing up on the streets of Brooklyn, New York, he and his best friend, James "Bucky" Barnes, had gotten into their fair share of fights. But it was usually Bucky who managed to keep them safe. Steve was scrappy, but physically he wasn't anything to write home about. He was skinny and frail, and because of his asthma, he couldn't even do enough exercise to add some muscles. He also had other health problems. The list was so long doctors usually thought he was making some of them up. But that was the last thing in the world Steve Rogers was going to do. He would have done anything to be fit for the army.

Not every soldier had to be a muscleman, like Johnny Weissmuller or Charles Atlas. You could win wars with brains and heart. Steve had enough brains, he figured, and he had a big heart. Some army recruitment center would eventually give him what he wanted most—a 1A stamp. Then he could be a US soldier, like his father had been. Which is why he now stood in line in the fifth recruitment center in the fifth city, hoping this would be the day. He knew it was not exactly legal to try to enlist in multiple locations, but so far, no one seemed to have caught on.

"Rogers, Steven?" a voice called out, startling Steve.

He stepped forward, wiping his hands nervously on his pants.

The doctor opened his file and began to scan it. "Father died of...?"

"Mustard gas," Steve said. He wasn't sad about it anymore. He was proud of his father's service, and he kept his head high as he said it. "He was with the One

Hundred and Seventh Infantry. I was hoping I could be assigned—"

"Mother?"

This one hurt a little more. "She was a nurse in a TB ward," Steve said. "Got hit. Couldn't shake it."

Not that anyone ever shook tuberculosis, not really. Steve had been an orphan for a while now. But he was doing all right on his own.

The doctor kept going through the file, his eyes growing wide as he took in all the ailments that had been checked off. The paper looked like it had been attacked by a red pen.

"Just give me a chance," Steve said.

"Sorry, son," the doctor said, looking up at him. "You'd be ineligible on your asthma alone."

He didn't say it, but Steve knew what he was thinking. *You're a fool, kid. The war is for strong men. Not for guys like you. Not for guys who can't even breathe right.*

"You can't do anything?" Steve asked anyway, hope in his voice.

"I'm doing it," the doctor answered. "I'm saving your life."

Then, as Steve watched, the doctor pulled out the dreaded stamp. With a resounding thunk, he pressed it down on the file, marking it with a big black *4F*.

Steve had failed—again.

A short while later, Steve was back in Brooklyn, inside a darkened movie theater. Up on the screen, images from the front lines flashed by in a newsreel. There was a picture of a bombed-out town, followed by images of soldiers pulling wounded men out of the line of fire. Another image showed the enemy marching into an undefended town, knocking down people and buildings as they went.

Nearby, Steve heard the unmistakable sound of someone crying. So many people had already lost loved ones or were about to send them off to the front lines. Steve didn't have anybody who would miss him if he went. His parents were gone, and his closest friend, Bucky, had already enlisted and was being shipped off the next day. Bucky would be over in Europe in no time, doing his part for the war effort, while Steve stayed behind. Useless.

The sound of an angry voice broke through Steve's

thoughts. "Who cares? Play the movie already!" someone shouted from behind him.

Steve's eyes narrowed. What kind of guy would say something like that at a time like this? He turned in his seat and tried to see who had spoken, but the screen had gone dark for a moment and it was difficult to make out anyone in the shadows. "Can you keep it down, please?" he asked quietly, hoping that the person with the bad attitude would hear him.

But apparently he didn't, because a moment later the guy called out, "Let 'em clean up their own mess!"

Steve shot out of his seat. He had had enough. "You want to shut up, pal?" he asked, turning around. Then Steve's eyes grew wide. In the light of the screen, he could now see who was talking. The guy was huge, and he looked way too eager to fight.

Steve gulped. What had he gotten himself into?

In the alley behind the theater, Steve stood with his fists in front of him. Balancing on the balls of his feet, he bobbed and weaved from side to side, trying to look tough. But the other guy was easily double his size, with fists the size of Steve's head.

The big guy advanced toward Steve, who leaped forward, hitting him with an uppercut and then getting a good punch into his kidney. The hit made the man flinch—but only for a moment. He came back at Steve, swinging his meaty fists. Steve ducked one punch and then another. He stepped lightly back and out of the way as the guy swung again. Smiling, Steve tried to get another hit in.

But then his luck ran out. He tried to punch the guy but got too close, and in one quick move, the big man knocked Steve flat with a roundhouse right. Steve got up and came after him again, and the big guy knocked him down again. This time Steve had a split lip. He spat blood on the alley bricks and got his guard up again.

"You just don't know when to give up, do you?" the big guy said.

"I can do this all day," Steve panted.

Struggling to get back the wind that had been knocked out of him, Steve unsteadily got to his feet. He shook his head, trying to clear his vision. The guy let out a mean laugh. He made a fist, pulled back his arm—and just as he went to swing, someone grabbed his bicep, stopping him and momentarily saving Steve.

"Hey, pick on someone your own size." Steve opened his eyes, which he had shut in anticipation of the punch, and smiled. He knew that voice. Bucky had arrived. It wasn't the first time Bucky had bailed out his best friend. He smiled as he spoke to the meathead, but it wasn't a friendly smile. When he let the guy's arm go, the guy took a swing at him. Bucky slipped the punch and decked him, careful not to muss up his spotless dress uniform. The smile never left his face. The guy headed for the mouth of the alley. Bucky gave him a swift kick in the behind to make sure he went a little faster. The grin on his face got more friendly as he took in Steve.

"Sometimes I think you like getting punched," he said.

Making his way over to Steve, Bucky helped him to his feet. Then he reached down to pick up a slip of paper that had fallen out of Steve's jacket. Seeing what it was, he stifled a groan. It was another recruitment slip. He knew how much his friend wanted to be a soldier, but he also knew that it was probably not going to happen. And while Bucky would never say anything out loud, it made him sort of mad. True, he wanted to help his country win the war. But he was going to be shipped out tomorrow, and he was nervous. He didn't know what to expect across the ocean, and a part of him wished he had the same excuse Steve did.

Sighing, he handed the slip of paper back to Steve. "Now you're from Paramus?" he asked. "You know it's illegal to lie on an enlistment form, don't you?"

Steve shrugged. "You get your orders?" he asked. Bucky couldn't possibly understand what it was like to be him. Even now, standing in the dirty alley, Bucky looked like a hero—something Steve could never be.

"Sergeant James Barnes, shipping out for England first thing tomorrow." He saw that cut into Steve a little, and he felt bad about it.

Seeing the sadness in Steve's eyes, Bucky decided to drop the subject. Time was precious now, and it seemed silly to waste it being in a bad mood. He had another idea.

"Come on, man. My last night. Gotta get you cleaned off."

"Why?" Steve asked. "Where are we going?"

"The future," Bucky said. Holding up a newspaper, he smiled. On the front page was a picture of the fairgrounds with a headline that read: 1942 WORLD EXHIBITION OF TOMORROW.

Steve raised a curious eyebrow. Bucky wanted to go to a fair? Now? Shrugging, he followed his friend out of the alley. Maybe going to see an exhibition about "tomorrow" would help him forget all about today.

CHAPTER 2

A few hours later, Bucky and Steve made their way onto the fairgrounds. At some point, Bucky had managed to find two young ladies to accompany them and was busy trying to get Steve to talk with one of them. But it wasn't working. Steve was too busy taking in the sights, particularly the Modern Marvels pavilion.

The fairgrounds looked like something out of a science-fiction novel. Huge, futuristic buildings had been erected, and they stood alongside smaller tents and pavilions. High above the ground, a monorail silently glided by, carrying passengers from one end of the exposition to the other. People of all ages wandered around, their eyes wide open at the various sights. Steve had to admit it was pretty amazing.

Making their way farther into the fair, Steve and Bucky noticed a commotion over to one side. Walking closer, they saw a big sign that read: STARK INDUSTRIES. Standing on a raised platform next to a very expensive car was a man Steve recognized from the papers— Howard Stark. He was a millionaire inventor and notorious playboy who was always photographed out on the town with a beautiful woman on his arm. Right now he was giving some kind of spiel about "gravitic-reversion technology," whatever that was. "What if I told you that, in a few short years, your car won't even have to touch the ground at all?" he called out over the crowd. There were some catcalls and some cheers.

As they watched, Stark smiled and pulled a lever. Suddenly the car lifted up off the ground. It was floating and its wheels moved so they were parallel to the ground! The audience oohed and aahed, taking in the sight of the car of tomorrow. But then a series of loud pops and a shower of sparks came out of the wheel wells and the car dropped back to the ground, shaking the platform. Stark just smiled again and began talking about how not even he was perfect. "Well, I did say a few years, didn't I?" he said, spreading his arms and with the kind of smile that said he'd be right back at it again tomorrow.

Turning to say something to Steve, Bucky noticed that his friend was no longer by his side. Even Steve's date didn't know where he had gone. Sighing, Bucky went to look for him.

He found Steve standing in front of the one non-futuristic pavilion in the entire fair, the US Army recruitment booth. It looked empty. No one wanted to think about the war now, not when they could think about all the amazing things the future held. No one but Steve Rogers. He stood staring at the tent, enraptured.

"You're really going to do this now?" Bucky asked, walking over to stand next to him.

"I'm going to try my luck," Steve said, nodding.

"As who?" Bucky said, his voice harsh. "'Steve from Ohio'? They'll catch you. Or worse, they'll actually take you."

That was it. Bucky had had enough. He was leaving for England tomorrow, and his best friend in the world wouldn't take the night off to have some fun with him, talk with some pretty girls, and maybe have a dance or two.

It was the first time Bucky had ever voiced his fears about Steve fighting in the war. Steve was taken aback by his friend's honesty.

"This isn't a back-alley scrap, Steve," Bucky continued, his voice softening. "It's a war."

"No," Steve corrected. "It's *the* war. The war we can't lose. This is the one that counts—and I mean to be counted."

Steve took a step toward the tent, and Bucky put a hand on his arm as one of the girls called out, "Hey, Bucky, are we going dancing or what?"

"We sure are," Bucky called back. "Come on," he said to Steve. "It's my last night."

His friend turned and gave him a wry smile. There was nothing Bucky could say or do that would convince Steve to leave that pavilion. Holding out his hand, he and Steve shook. It was time to say good-bye.

"Don't do anything stupid until I get back," Bucky said.

"How can I? You're taking all the stupid with you," Steve said. "Don't win the war 'til I get there." Then he walked away toward the tent.

Bucky watched his friend go, his heart heavy. He hoped, for Steve's sake, that he would get what he wanted. He just wasn't convinced that when Steve got it, it would make him happy.

There was a part of Steve that knew he was being ridiculous. How many more times could he fail? And it was Bucky's last night. But if there was even the slimmest chance that his luck could change, then he had to take it.

Walking inside the recruitment center, he was directed to an examination room. His eyes quickly adjusted to the dark. Where outside it was all bright lights and noisy crowds, inside it was quiet and somber.

Out of the corner of his eye, Steve saw an older man come in. He looked tired, as though being there took all his energy.

The man made his way slowly over to Steve. "So. You want to go overseas? Be a hero?" he asked in a German accent. Steve just looked at him. He wasn't sure what to say. Was this some kind of test?

"Dr. Abraham Erskine," the man said, introducing himself. "Strategic Scientific Reserve, US Army."

Steve had never heard of the Strategic Scientific Reserve but figured there were a lot of things he hadn't heard of. Shrugging, he gave Erskine his name and looked on as the man found his file. Steve tried not to grimace when he once again saw all the red x's, marking each and every one of his ailments and weaknesses.

"Where are you from?" he asked, to draw the doctor's attention away from the file.

"Queens," Erskine said. He paused, then added, "Before that, Germany. This bothers you?"

Steve was momentarily taken aback. Was this place legit? He hadn't expected a German national to be inside a US Army recruitment center.

Then again, wasn't Einstein German, too? "No," he said, but he hesitated first.

It didn't seem to bother Erskine. Probably he'd heard it all before. He finished reviewing the file and then looked up. "Where are you from, Mr. Rogers?" he asked. "Hmm? New Haven? Or is it..." He glanced down at the file again. "Paramus... Newark... five exams in five tries in five different cities," he said. "All failed. You are very tenacious, yes?"

How did he know that? Steve wondered. He'd thought that by going to different cities, he could stay under the radar and the army wouldn't see how desperate he was to enlist. Maybe this Strategic Scientific Reserve, whatever it was, had more intel than the other branches of the army.

Outside, a pair of men wandered by and turned when they heard Erskine's German accent. They took a step forward as though to do something, when Steve held up a warning hand. Figuring it wasn't worth it, they moved on.

"A fella has to stand up," Steve said, turning back to Erskine. "I don't like bullies, Doc. I don't care where they're from."

The old man nodded thoughtfully. "So you would fight, yes," he said. "But you are weak and you are very small."

Steve was about to protest, when Dr. Erskine did something unexpected: He laid out Steve's file on the table and picked up a stamp. Steve's heart began to beat faster.

"I can offer you a chance," Dr. Erskine said. "Only a chance."

Then, as Steve watched with growing excitement, the man pressed the stamp down on the file. Holding up the file, Steve saw a big *1A*.

He couldn't believe it. After all this time, he was actually in the army. His luck *had* changed. Just like he told Bucky it would.

As Erskine began talking about next steps, Steve tried to pay attention. But his mind was spinning. He had no idea what kind of group the SSR was or why they would okay someone like him. Should he be worried? Was Bucky right when he said the biggest danger would come if someone *did* let him in? What if this was all some sort of joke? Maybe when he got outside he'd see Bucky laughing, having pulled a fast one on his old friend.

Shaking off those thoughts, Steve focused on Erskine. Whatever the SSR was and whatever the reason they had for taking him, Steve didn't care. He was in. Soon, he would be a real soldier, and maybe, someday, he'd even be an American hero.

CHAPTER 3

Steve Rogers wasn't the only one chosen by the Strategic Scientific Reserve. A few days later he found himself standing in line at Camp Lehigh in the practice field with eleven other recruits. They were all healthy and tall and strong, and next to them, Steve felt even smaller than he usually did. But that didn't stop him from signing the last-will-and-testament document without a moment's hesitation. While the other recruits were all nervous about signing their lives away, Steve was willing to give all that he could to the US Army, even if it meant his own life.

Steve and the rest of the recruits filed into a large room, where Steve spied a man and a woman, watching and waiting. The man scowled at Steve, who was relieved to see Dr. Erskine off to one side, observing the recruits. The other man then introduced himself as Colonel Chester Phillips. He stood ramrod straight, multiple medals shining on his uniform. Deep lines were etched on his face, marking the combat missions that he had survived. Yet his eyes were still bright, clear, and serious as they surveyed the room.

Colonel Phillips addressed the men: "The Strategic Scientific Reserve is an Allied effort, made up of the best minds in the free world," he began. With that, the colonel then introduced Dr. Erskine and Agent Peggy Carter, who was on loan to the army from British Intelligence, and, despite her obvious beauty, looked only slightly less intimidating than Colonel Phillips.

When Agent Carter began to speak, Steve noticed that there was a lot of quiet chuckling and chattering going on. The recruits kept eyeing Peggy, taking in her long legs and pretty face. They also questioned why they were being addressed by a British officer. "I thought I was signing up for the US Army," one of them said.

Agent Carter stopped talking and zeroed in on him. Steve had just met him. He was a big, rawboned blond guy named Hodge. "What's your name, soldier?" she asked. Hodge told her. "Put your right foot forward," she instructed him.

"Why? What kind of move is a dame gonna teach me?" Hodge asked, loud enough for the whole group of recruits to hear.

Peggy decked him with a straight right to the nose. Then she straightened herself, cool and collected, while Hodge started to get up. Blood ran from his nose.

"Agent Carter," the colonel said.

She came to attention. "Colonel Phillips."

"I can see you're breaking in the candidates," the colonel said. He gave Hodge a hard glare as Hodge got to his feet and back in the muster line. "That's good."

The breaking-in didn't stop there. It was only getting started. First up was the obstacle course. As he stood waiting for his team's turn, Steve tried to remember everything he had read about obstacle courses. He knew that they were supposed to help a soldier learn how to handle combat situations while building a sense of team camaraderie. But looking out over the various objects on the course, and then taking in the men standing on either side of him, he doubted that would happen. The obstacles included a climbing wall, rope swings, a rappelling wall, a long piece of wood that looked like a balance beam but with a rough surface, large rubber tires, and even a deep mud puddle.

The men already on the course raced through the obstacles, easily climbing over the wall and nimbly running across the balance beam. It looked as if they had been doing this sort of thing their whole lives.

"Our goal is to create the finest army in history," Colonel Phillips said as they waited. "But every army starts with one man. By the end of this week, we're going to choose that man. He's going to be the first of a new breed of Super-Soldiers."

Super-Soldiers? Steve repeated silently. Was there something going on he didn't know about? But he didn't have time to think about it, as a horn sounded, signaling his turn to go. He leaped at the wall, trying to pull himself over, but one of the other men's boots landed squarely on his head, pushing him back. By the time he made it over, he was way behind the others. He could see Phillips, Peggy, and Erskine watching and increased his speed. But he knew that he'd already made a bad impression. He had to pick up his game.

Erskine turned to Phillips, his mind made up. "Rogers is the clear choice," he told the colonel. But Phillips couldn't disagree more.

"You put a needle in that guy's arm," the colonel began, "it's going to come out the other side."

Phillips continued to watch Steve, who was once again the last in line. "Look at him," Phillips said to Erskine. "He's making me cry."

But the course continued, and so did Steve. He scrambled up a cargo net only to get tangled in it when Hodge walked over him. But he recovered and kept going. He crawled through mud covered by barbed wire only to have Hodge kick out a support beam, causing the barbed wire to fall on Steve. Still, he kept going.

His efforts didn't go unnoticed.

Agent Carter and Dr. Erskine had seen Hodge try to sabotage Steve over and over again. And yet each time, Steve had gotten back up, more determined than ever. He didn't have the muscles of the other recruits, but he had something they didn't—heart. He would fight as hard as he could as long as he could and never turn a back on a fellow soldier. Those were the qualities Peggy and Erskine were looking for. Phillips, however, didn't feel the same way. He still saw Steve as a weak, ineffectual soldier-in-training.

Phillips wanted Hodge for the job and wasted no time in voicing his opinion. "He's big, he's fast, he takes orders. In short, he's a soldier."

"No," Erskine interjected. "He's a bully."

Phillips immediately countered Erskine's argument. "You don't win wars with niceness, Doctor. You win them with guts." And to prove his point, Phillips picked up a grenade and hurled it into the middle of the course, right near Steve.

As Hodge and the other recruits panicked and fled, Steve ran right at the grenade. "Everybody, down!"

he shouted as he flung himself on top of the explosive device.

There was a moment of silence as everyone waited for the inevitable. One second passed. Two seconds. Three. Finally, Steve gingerly eased himself up and off the grenade. Looking over to where Phillips, Peggy, and Erskine stood, he cocked his head and asked, "Is this a test?"

Peggy tried not to smile. It was a test of sorts, and not even Colonel Phillips could deny that Steve had passed. Erskine cocked an eyebrow at the colonel. "He's still skinny," Phillips growled. But he didn't argue any more. The SSR didn't need to look any further: Steve Rogers was going to be their first Super-Soldier.

Later that night, Steve sat alone inside the barracks. The rest of the recruits had been sent home, and the empty beds made Steve feel even more alone. But a part of him was excited about what the future held. Peggy and Dr. Erskine had given him more details once he was chosen; he was to be given a special serum that Erskine had created. With luck, it would turn him into a man with extraordinary powers. He'd be able to run faster, hit harder, and think quicker—all things that would be helpful on the battlefield. But there would also be risks in undergoing such a procedure—namely, would he survive the experiment?

The sound of footsteps echoed in the empty room, and Steve looked up. Erskine had entered the barracks and was walking toward him. As always, the doctor's expression was somber.

"Can I ask you a question?" Steve said when the older man took a seat on the bed across from him. Erskine nodded. "Why me?"

The doctor smiled. He had been expecting this question. And Steve deserved to know the answer—and the history behind the serum.

Five years ago, Erskine began, he was living in Germany working as a scientist. His experiments were radical, and some felt they were foolish. But then he had invented a serum that had the possibility of giving a man almost-superhuman abilities. It promised great power to anyone who controlled it and, as the war was just beginning, the potential for whoever had it to be victorious. Erskine was eager to keep it out of the wrong hands—but then a man named Johann Schmidt found out about his discovery.

Schmidt, Erskine explained, was himself a brilliant scientist, and also the leader of an organization called Hydra. At the time that Erskine worked with him, Schmidt was fascinated with occult powers and Teutonic myths. So was Hitler. Steve knew that. But Schmidt wasn't a true believer, a real Nazi. He longed for his own glory, no matter what the cost. Schmidt believed that worlds existed in which men had the strength of gods and could control weather and the elements. He became obsessed with the idea that a great power had been hidden on Earth by the gods and was waiting to be seized by a superior man. Schmidt—and Hydra—vowed to find that power.

Steve raised an eyebrow and Erskine nodded as if to say, *yes, insane, I know.* Then he continued.

Schmidt believed that Erskine's serum was the key to that power. And he wanted it. Despite Erskine's every attempt to stop him, Schmidt got his hands on the serum and, in an act of desperation, injected himself.

The results were horrific, and the experiment was a failure.

Erskine had no choice. He fled his country and made his way to the United States in the hope of keeping the rest of the serum out of Schmidt's hands. But he knew that the Hydra leader would never stop looking for him—or the serum. The failed experiment had corrupted Schmidt, and in Erskine's eyes, it had turned the scientist into a monster.

"This is why you were chosen," Erskine said to Steve, who had been listening intently. "A strong man, he might lose respect for power if he had it all his life. But a weak man knows the value of strength...and compassion."

The scientist sighed deeply. He saw the doubt in Steve's eyes and couldn't blame him. It was a rather unbelievable story. But it was an important one. For Erskine had learned a valuable lesson.

"The serum amplifies what is inside," he finished. "Good becomes great. Bad becomes worse." Erskine looked Steve straight in the eyes. "Whatever happens tomorrow," he said, "promise me you'll stay who you are. Not a perfect soldier, but a good man."

Steve nodded in silence. Tomorrow was going to be a very interesting day. He just hoped that Erskine and Peggy were right about him. He didn't want to think about what would happen if they were wrong.

CHAPTER 4

The next day Peggy picked up Steve early in the morning and took him away from Camp Lehigh. They soon found themselves driving through the streets of Brooklyn, New York. For the first time since the night of the exhibition, his thoughts drifted to Bucky and to their misspent youth on the streets.

"I know this neighborhood," Steve said to Peggy. "I got beat up in that alley." He pointed out the car window. "And over there," he added, pointing to a corner outside a soda fountain. "And there." This time he nodded at a side street blocked by a garbage truck.

Peggy looked at him quizzically. "Did you have something against running away?" she asked.

"You start running," Steve began, "they'll never let you stop. You stand up, you push back...They can only tell you no for so long, right?"

Peggy smiled to herself, more confident than ever that the SSR had made the right choice in picking Steve Rogers.

The car came to a stop, jolting Steve. Looking around, he saw that they had parked in front of an antiques store.

"Why did we stop here?" he asked, confused.

"I love a bargain," she answered simply, opening the car door and getting out. Steve laughed. Peggy was full of surprises, and he felt a weird flutter in his chest. He hated to admit it, but he was starting to like Peggy.

Getting out of the car, he followed her inside. An old woman stood behind the counter, surrounded by various knickknacks and dusty antiques. "Wonderful weather this morning," Peggy said.

"Isn't it?" the shopkeeper said.

"Yes, but I always carry an umbrella."

The woman nodded at Peggy, then pressed a hidden button, allowing Peggy and Steve to enter. This was serious spy stuff. Steve couldn't quite believe it all.

At a door in the back of the store, Peggy stopped and turned to make sure Steve was behind her. Then she opened the door, revealing a secret staircase. They made their way down and walked through another door— right into the Strategic Scientific Reserve Rebirth lab.

Steve's eyes grew wide as he took in the giant space. Far larger than the store above, it was illuminated by bright lights and bustling with activity. In the center of the ultramodern area, technicians operated different kinds of machinery, consulting with one another as they pulled levers and flipped switches. A group of engineers manned a row of monitors that beeped with information, while in another part of the lab a film crew was setting up their equipment.

Looking up, Steve noticed an observation booth. Several serious-looking men stood inside talking. Peggy quickly informed him that the man with the salt-and-pepper hair was Senator Brandt. He had helped the SSR get funding for the serum experiment—code-named Project: Rebirth—and was here to see if his money had been well spent.

As Steve walked farther into the lab, everyone turned to stare at him. He smiled self-consciously when he realized that he might be in over his head. Instinctively, he made his way to Dr. Erskine, who stood next to a large mechanical assembly. It was centered around a kind of human-shaped recess, almost like a cradle. Surrounding it were rows of brackets and straps and all kinds of medical-looking instruments and machines. This, Erskine informed him, was the Rebirth device. It was in this cradle that Steve would be given the serum.

With a deep breath, Steve got inside. It was now or never.

"Comfortable?" Dr. Erskine asked.

At Steve's nod, Erskine smiled. Then, turning to the attendants standing at the ready, he gave them the signal. They began to hook up Steve to various wires, tubes, and monitors. These would help Erskine observe Steve's reactions as the experiment proceeded.

"How are your levels, Mr. Stark?" Erskine asked, turning to someone Steve hadn't noticed before.

The man turned and Steve raised an eyebrow. It was Howard Stark, the inventor he had seen at the World Exhibition of Tomorrow. Stark wasn't a military man, so he must also be on loan to the SSR, Steve thought.

"Coils are at peak," Stark replied to Erskine. "Levels are one hundred percent. We're ready." Then he paused before adding, "As we'll ever be."

Erskine didn't seem as concerned. Picking up a microphone that would carry his words into the observation booth, he began to speak. "Today, we take the first step on the path to peace," he said. Behind him, more attendants fiddled with the machines hooked up to Steve. A heart monitor began to beep in time with Steve's racing heart.

"The serum will cause immediate cellular change," Erskine went on. "In order to prevent uncontrolled growth, the subject will then be saturated with Vita-Rays."

Uncontrolled growth? Saturated with rays? The heart monitor started beeping faster as Steve listened. So his cradle was going to turn into a chamber? And he'd be shot full of rays? *If Bucky were here right now,* Steve thought, *he'd tell me, "I told you so."*

Turning off the microphone, Erskine nodded to a nurse. She opened up a case, revealing an aluminum syringe. She tapped it a few times, pulled back the plunger, and injected Steve in the arm.

"That wasn't so bad," Steve said when she was done.

"*That* was penicillin," Erskine said, a small smile on his face.

As Steve looked on, a panel slid back, revealing a carousel of blue vials. There were seven tubes of serum in total. Erskine and the nurse began inserting the vials one by one into the injectors set up around Steve. When they had inserted six of the seven, Erskine had another technician move closer. He was in charge of the injector pads—small round objects covered with hundreds of tiny needle tips. They were lightly placed all over the outside of Steve's body. When they were pressed down into his skin, the serum would flow through the injectors, into the pads, and then into Steve.

Then Erskine began the countdown. "Beginning serum infusion in five, four, three, two...one."

He pressed a switch, and Steve jerked as the pads pressed down on him. The blue fluid flowed from the injectors. Instantly, Steve's veins began to swell and his head began to shake as the fluid washed through him.

Erskine hit another button and padded restraints closed around Steve's head, calming the shaking. But it didn't stop his eyes from glowing blue. From the look on Erskine's face, though, it seemed as if this was supposed to happen.

When the six vials were finally empty, Erskine turned to the millionaire inventor. "Now, Mr. Stark."

Stark pulled a lever, and the cradle began to tilt. When it was finished moving, Steve was straight up, and the cradle looked like a rocket ready to launch. Then a panel slid across the cradle, sealing Steve inside. Through a small window, everyone could see Steve's face. With the panels closed, the cradle was now ready to be flooded with Vita-Rays, which would hopefully keep Steve safe. The Vita-Ray machine came courtesy of

Howard Stark, who gave Steve a reassuring nod before moving to the control device.

A piercing whine filled the air as Stark turned a power dial. On a big gauge, a needle began to climb, indicating the level of rays flooding the chamber. It hit ten, then twenty. Steve's face began to tense. At forty, his eyes squeezed shut. Then the needle reached sixty, and the heart monitor began beeping wildly. The rays were affecting Steve badly. Stark looked to Erskine, ready to turn the machine off, but the scientist shook his head. They had to keep going.

The needle reached eighty, and a strange orange glow filled the device chamber. Steve's face could no longer be seen through the window. Inside, Steve was completely unaware of what was going on as the rays battered his body. Outside, Erskine's own heart pounded. He knew he was putting Steve in great danger, but he had to....

When the needle hit ninety, Steve let out a piercing scream. Up in the booth, Brandt and his aides took a step back when they heard it. On the lab floor, Erskine watched as the orange light grew even brighter. It was too much. "Kill the reactors!" he ordered.

Stark was about to turn the dial down when over the microphone came Steve's voice, faint but determined. "No," he said. "I can do this."

Erskine swallowed. They had chosen Steve because he had heart, and it seemed he was determined to see this through. The doctor hesitated and then finally nodded at Stark. The other man gave the dial a final turn. One hundred. A sharp whine split the air, and the chamber flashed from orange to white.

Then everything went dark.

Silence filled the lab. The heart monitor stopped beeping and no sound came from inside the chamber. Up in the booth, Brandt looked down at Erskine, his expression a mixture of disappointment and anger. Everyone in the room held their breath in anticipation.

Then, suddenly, the heart monitor came to life. *Beep, beep, beep.*

Anxious, Erskine took a step forward. Had it worked? Was it possible?

There was only one way to tell. Stark opened the chamber.

Scientists peered through the smoke and machinery

as the chamber cleared of the last rays. And then, Erskine smiled.

Steve was still strapped into the chamber. But it wasn't the same Steve who had gone in. No longer was he thin and frail. Instead, he was now a model of human perfection, standing a foot taller than before, with muscles rippling all over his new body. Project: Rebirth had worked!

"You did it, Doctor!" Stark shouted as he unstrapped Steve, who was momentarily weakened from the ordeal. "You really did it!"

As Stark helped Steve over to a chair, everyone rushed in, eager to see the results and congratulate one another. In the middle of the excitement, Steve sat, taking everything in. He felt different. He couldn't tell what he looked like, but from the reactions of those around him, he figured it was good. And from the reaction of Peggy, he figured it was *very* good. "How do you feel?" she asked.

"Taller," he said, looking down at her as he smiled.

Peggy smiled back. At least his spirits hadn't changed.

And then everything started to go downhill—fast.

While they were talking, one of the men who had been in the observation booth made his way into the lab. He wore glasses and went by the name Fred Clemson. Ignoring Dr. Erskine and the others, he made his way to the chamber—and the last remaining vial of serum. Glancing quickly around to make sure no one was looking, he pulled out a lighter. With a flick of his thumb, he opened it, revealing a button instead of the usual wick.

Erskine heard the sound through the chatter in the lab and turned. He knew that sound. His eyes grew wide. He also knew that person. His name wasn't Fred Clemson. His name was Kruger, and he was a Hydra agent. Erskine saw Kruger at the same time the other man saw him. An evil smile spread across Kruger's face, and his thumb pressed down on the lighter. Then he threw it.

"No!" Erskine shouted. But it was too late. The observation room exploded.

CHAPTER 5

Everything was going according to Hydra's plan. Kruger had infiltrated the Strategic Scientific Reserve's headquarters just as he'd been instructed. And he had at least partially destroyed their lab, just as he'd been told. Now he needed to get his hands on the last remaining vial of serum and make his escape.

Through the smoke, Kruger saw Erskine, who was still seen as a traitor by the Hydra organization.

Pulling out his pistol, Kruger aimed and fired. Erskine went down. Grabbing the vial, Kruger headed for the door.

Hearing the shot, Steve looked up. He was still shaky from the experiment—and the explosion—and his limbs felt out of sync with the rest of his body. But when Steve saw Erskine fall, he jumped to his feet and raced over to his friend. But it was too late. Erskine was mortally wounded. He locked eyes with Steve and tried to speak. One of his hands came up, like he was going to grab Steve's shirt...but then he tapped Steve hard just to the left of his sternum. Right over his heart.

Steve nodded. He thought he understood.

Erskine's eyes moved toward the door. He was having trouble focusing them, Steve could see that. Erskine managed to whisper the name "Kruger," and then his eyes closed.

For a moment, Steve didn't know what to do. Erskine was dead. The lab was in shambles. And a spy was racing off with the last vial of serum. How had everything gone from so good to so terribly bad in such a short amount of time? Shaking his head, Steve saw Kruger heading for the second door. Kruger turned his gun on the old woman behind the counter. She was reaching for her machine gun, but the Hydra agent was faster. He made his way out of the antiques shop.

But Steve wasn't going to let him get away. Jumping to his feet, he took off after the agent. When Steve burst out onto the street, he was just in time to see Kruger pulling the driver out of a taxicab. He threw the poor man to the ground and jumped into the cab. Peggy, who had also chased after Kruger, pulled out a gun and opened fire. Kruger returned fire, hitting a car behind Peggy, causing it to explode into flames. Then, with a squeal of tires, Kruger peeled out and raced away.

Peggy thought the Hydra spy would get away. Until she saw Steve.

Steve Rogers was now very fast. Superfast. He charged after Kruger, running as quickly as his new legs could carry him. Kruger drove down an alley, then turned and kept going, with Steve just a few feet behind. With a huge roar, Steve launched himself at the taxi, landing with a thud on the roof. Behind the glass, Kruger's eyes narrowed and he raised his arm. He still held his pistol. With a smile, he fired, shattering the cab's window. Steve ducked to the side. His grip loosened and he fell, clinging with all his might to the cab.

The buildings rushed by as Kruger drove on, heading toward the Brooklyn piers. Suddenly, up in front, Kruger saw a truck roaring toward him. He jerked the wheel, but it was too late. The truck sideswiped the cab, sending it—and Steve—into a roll. The world spun upside down as the cab flipped over and over again, finally coming to a stop, its hood smoking.

As Steve struggled to his feet, Kruger stumbled out of the wreckage, gun firing. Steve ducked, but the bullets were flying too fast. Thinking quickly, he grabbed a cab door that had been knocked loose and held it up in front of him like a shield. The bullets bounced off the metal, ricocheting harmlessly. Kruger kept firing.

Their high-speed ride had taken them right down to the piers, which, on the sunny day, were filled with civilians catching the sights and enjoying the afternoon. Seeing the commotion, some of them began snapping pictures of the gunfight, mistaking it for entertainment.

Then Kruger turned, shoving pedestrians aside as he ran.

Seeing a young boy among the gathering crowd, Kruger grabbed him and pulled him to his chest, holding the gun to the boy's head. Steve slowed down as Kruger began moving backward toward the water. When he was close enough to jump, Kruger threw the boy into the water and pulled out a small device. He clicked a button and a small one-man submarine surfaced a few feet away. Kruger gave Steve an evil smile and then scrambled into the Hydra sub.

Steve looked down at the water. He couldn't let Kruger get away, but he also couldn't let the little boy drown.

"Go get him!" the boy shouted, interrupting Steve's thoughts. "I can swim."

"Great," Steve muttered, more to himself than the kid. "I can't."

But he had no choice. The boy was okay and Kruger had to be stopped. Taking a deep breath, Steve ran to the edge of the pier and jumped, landing in the chilly water. The cold knocked the air out of Steve's lungs, and for a moment he wondered if he was going to drown in spite of his newfound superpowers. But then his legs began to kick of their own accord, and before he knew it he was slicing through the water with long, powerful strokes. In no time, he had caught up to the sub. Reaching out, he grabbed its tail fin. Pulling himself forward, hand over hand, he made it to the cockpit. Through the glass, he saw Kruger's eyes widen at the sight of him. Then Steve pulled back his fist and punched the glass over and over again. With a mighty crack, it broke, allowing water to rush inside.

Reaching into the cockpit, Steve grabbed Kruger and yanked him free of the now-sinking sub. Then, with another mighty kick, he headed toward the surface.

Back on dry land, he threw Kruger to the ground. But the Hydra soldier wouldn't give up. He pulled out a knife and tried to stab the American. Steve effortlessly kicked the knife aside. As he lunged at Kruger, the vial of blue serum broke, the fluid spilling onto the stones of the wharf.

"Who are you?" Steve yelled.

"The first of many," he said cryptically. Then Kruger pressed his tongue against a false tooth, triggering a cyanide pill. "Cut off one head and two more shall rise." His body began to shake and his mouth started to foam. Right before Kruger died, he said, "Hail Hydra."

Steve sat there for a long time after Kruger died, his mind racing. What sort of organization would send someone like Kruger to kill Erskine and harm innocent people? And now that they had failed to get their hands on the serum, would they also come after Steve?

Later, back at the SSR HQ, Peggy sat down with Steve to brief him on the situation. He'd known it was bad because they'd lost Erskine, but after talking with Peggy for only a few minutes, Steve started to understand just how bad.

"All of Dr. Erskine's research and equipment is gone. Any hope of reproducing the project is locked away in your genetic code." She put her hand on Steve's shoulder. "At the moment, you're the only Super-Soldier there is," she said.

It was a strange feeling, to go from the skinny kid nobody wanted to the only survivor of some kind of crazy science-fiction experiment. What would happen next?

CHAPTER 6

The next day, Colonel Phillips and Senator Brandt were in the middle of a heated discussion. Phillips paced back and forth, his expression furious. They had been attacked on their own soil by an enemy spy who had managed to sneak in with the senator's entourage. It was a disgrace. And now, on top of it, Erskine was dead, and with him any hope of creating more Super-Soldiers. If Hydra had gotten their hands on that one vial...Phillips shivered at the thought. The SSR had only one option—go after Hydra before they came back after them.

As Phillips paced, Steve entered the headquarters. He had changed into a clean set of clothes that actually fit, but he looked tired from the events of the past few days.

Seeing him, Phillips grew even angrier. "I asked for an army!" he fumed. "All I got is you. And you are *not* enough."

Steve's head dipped as shame rushed over him. He felt like a failure. Everyone had put their faith in him, and he hadn't been able to keep Kruger from killing Erskine or taking the cyanide pill.

While Phillips exploded, Senator Brandt remained silent. Whereas the colonel was a ball of nerves, Brandt seemed eerily calm. He wasn't convinced that the experiment had been a failure. As if to prove it, he held up a copy of the day's paper. "You've seen Steve here in action," he said. "But more importantly, the *country's* seen it."

Walking closer, Phillips looked at the headline. It read: MYSTERY MAN SAVES CIVILIANS! Below it, there was an image taken of Steve the day before on the piers. He was using the cab door as a shield while Kruger fired.

Brandt waved the paper. "You don't take a soldier—a symbol—like this and hide him in a lab." Turning to Steve, he flashed his trademark smile, the one that had made him the successful senator he was. "Son, do you want to serve your country?" Steve nodded. "On the most important battlefield in this war?"

Of course Steve wanted to help. That was the whole reason he was in this situation in the first place. "It's all I want," he said.

The senator's smile got larger as he walked over and clapped Steve on the back. "Then congratulations. You just got promoted."

It didn't take long for Steve's promotion to go into effect. But it wasn't exactly what he'd been expecting.

A few days later, he found himself backstage in a small theater. His palms were sweaty, and he looked as if he was going to be sick to his stomach. One of Senator

Brandt's aides stood next to him, running through what was about to happen. Steve barely heard him.

"I don't think I can do this," he said softly. When Brandt had promised him that he would get to take part in the greatest battle of all, he had pictured being on the front lines, battling the enemy and saving his fellow soldiers. Not standing behind a curtain on a stage, preparing to do a song-and-dance act. But that was exactly what he was doing.

Before Steve could get any more nervous, the show began. The curtains parted, and a bugler walked onto the stage. He tilted his head back and blasted out reveille. Then, as the final notes faded, a band joined in and a line of girls danced across the stage, legs kicking high in the air. As Steve watched with a mixture of horror and embarrassment, they began to sing: "He's the star-spangled man with the star-spangled plan. He's Captain America!"

As they sang out the last word, Steve took a deep breath and moved forward. The aide had told him what to do. He was supposed to just walk through the flag and say his lines to the audience. But he felt like a fool.

He was dressed in what Senator Brandt had decided made him look most like "Captain America"—the war's newest hero—red boots and gloves, a pair of blue pants, and a shirt covered with stars and stripes. To top off the look, he had been given a mask with wings and a cheap red-white-and-blue shield. Steve had refused to look in the mirror, but he was mortified anyway. How was he supposed to inspire people to support the war looking like a kid in a Halloween costume? And what if the audience realized he'd never even set foot on the front line?

A shove from the aide reminded Steve that he hadn't moved. He stumbled forward past the flag and saw just a handful of kids sitting in the audience. So much for the big crowd Brandt had promised, Steve thought. Taking a deep breath, he eyed the cue card he had pasted on the back of his shield and began to speak. "Hello...uh, folks," he said. "Who here is ready to sock evil on the jaw?"

The kids let out a cheer, and Steve felt his shoulders relax. Maybe this wouldn't be so bad after all.

For the next few months, Steve traveled all over the

United States performing his Captain America show. At first, the crowds were small and Steve messed up—a lot. But slowly, things got better and the stages got bigger.

He went to Buffalo and tripped as the girls pulled him into their dance. In Milwaukee, he stayed on his feet and even managed to pose for photos with babies and their mothers. When he got to San Francisco, the stage was the biggest yet, and Steve felt proud when he walked through the flag and bent a pole into a red cross. With a smile, he handed it to a nurse in the audience and blushed when she batted her eyes at him.

The tour continued. Steve went to St. Louis and Chicago, where film crews recorded his act. Later that night, he saw himself on the big screen, and for the first time he began to believe that maybe Senator Brandt was onto something. Steve had never actually fought in the war, but what the public didn't know couldn't hurt them.

In Philadelphia, a young boy came up to him with pen and paper in hand. "Hey, Cap," he said, his eyes wide as he took in his hero, "my brother says you took out four German tanks all by yourself."

Steve patted the boy on the head. "Sorry, kid. Tell your brother he's wrong." The boy's eyes filled with disappointment until Steve added, "It was *eight* German tanks." As the boy cheered, Steve grinned.

He was beginning to believe his own hype. There were Captain America comics and photos. He was on the big screen, and he played to sold-out theaters. He was a bona fide hero. There was nothing he couldn't do.

And then Steve was sent to the front line.

CHAPTER 7

Captain America had taken his home country by storm, but Brandt wasn't satisfied. He wanted Steve to go to where the action was and energize the troops. Full of confidence and sure that he would be a star across the ocean, Steve flew over to Italy.

The US camp he was sent to was five miles from the front. When he got there, Steve took in the makeshift tents, the diverse troops, and the trucks that drove in and out at all hours carrying soldiers. It was nothing like the theaters and events back in America, where they didn't know the true horrors of war.

After changing into his costume, Steve took his spot in the wings and waited for the dancing girls to do their part. Then, as he had done countless times before, he stepped through the flag and shouted, "How many of you are ready to help me sock old Adolf in the jaw?"

He was met with silence.

Dozens of soldiers sat in their seats, glaring at him. Their uniforms were dirty and their faces lined with fatigue. Some of them had old wounds while others had fresh bandages on, having just returned from battle. Not one of them smiled at Steve.

Looking over his shoulder, he tried to find a way out. But there was no one waiting to signal him off the stage. So he forged on. "Okay," he said hesitantly, "I'm going to need a volunteer."

"I already volunteered," one of the soldiers shouted, his voice angry. "How do you think I got here?"

Steve opened his mouth to respond, when another soldier shouted, "Bring back the girls."

The crowd began to boo and jeer. Steve was taken aback. He had never experienced anything like this before.

As Steve retreated from the stage, the boos increased. Then tomatoes started flying. Holding up his shield, Steve blocked them. But it was a foolhardy effort. Even if none of the tomatoes hit him, he still felt like the biggest buffoon this side of the Atlantic.

A short while later, Steve sat in the empty bleachers, his head cradled in his hands. The soldiers had left, probably to go find real entertainment or talk about the real war and laugh at the man in the silly costume. Shame washed over Steve in huge waves. What had he been thinking? All this time he had fooled himself into believing he was a hero, a man of the people. But he was nothing but a joke. The men in the audience today were the real heroes. They had put their lives on the line time and time again, while all Steve had done was cheat his way to being a star. He hadn't even done anything with his superpowers since he had chased Kruger after the explosion. Had Erskine been wrong to think he was worthy? Had Phillips been right to doubt him?

The click of heels on the ground made Steve look up. He stifled a groan. Peggy Carter was walking toward him. He hadn't seen her since he had gone out on his "tour of duty," and he really didn't feel like seeing her now. She probably thought he was a joke, too. And he didn't want to see the disappointment in her beautiful eyes.

"What are you doing here?" he asked.

"Officially I'm not here at all," she replied. She took a seat next to him, and he met her gaze. He was surprised to see compassion there instead of disappointment, and his heart jumped in his chest. "That was quite a performance," she said, her voice gentle.

Steve shrugged. "The crowds I'm used to are usually more, uh..."

"I understand you're America's new hope," she said, quoting one of the many newspaper headlines about Captain America.

"Senator Brandt's idea," Steve said. "At least he's got me doing this. Phillips would have had me stuck in a lab." Then he sighed. He shouldn't take out his frustration on Peggy.

"And these are your only two options? A lab rat or a dancing monkey?"

"You know," he went on, "all I dreamed about was coming overseas, being with the men on the lines, seeing you. And I finally get everything I wanted...and I'm wearing tights."

For a moment, Peggy didn't say anything. She wouldn't admit it out loud, but Steve's words had made her heart beat faster. He had wanted to see her? Did that mean what she thought it meant?

Shaking her head, she smiled at Steve. "I thought you looked dashing, but I rather did have a thing for Errol Flynn in *Robin Hood*," she said with a gleam in her eyes.

"The worst part is," Steve said, so lost in his own misery that he missed Peggy's obvious flirtation, "I was starting to buy it."

"None of us thought it would turn out like this," Peggy said. "But you've done well."

Steve knew that Peggy was only trying to help. Still, he was tired of thinking about Captain America, because every time he did, a fresh wave of humiliation rolled over him. Changing the subject, he asked, "What about you?"

He had been kept vaguely informed of what Peggy and Phillips had been doing since Kruger attacked the lab. He knew that they'd been chasing Hydra. But he also knew that they had had little luck. From the look on Peggy's face, he knew the reports were right.

"We got word that Schmidt was moving a force through Azzano, testing some kind of new weaponry," she said after hesitating. "Two hundred men went in," she went on. "Fewer than fifty came back. Your adoring crowd tonight contained all that's left of the One Hundred and Seventh."

Steve sat bolt upright. "One Hundred and Seventh?" he repeated.

Peggy nodded. "Yes, why?"

He didn't bother to explain. Pulling her up, Steve began hurrying her down the bleachers, heading toward the tents. He had to see Colonel Phillips—now. The 107th had been his father's unit in the Great War. It was the unit he'd always wanted to get into, before he'd gotten sidetracked into this Super-Soldier business. But there was a more pressing reason for Steve's reaction to finding out that he was with the 107th now.

The 107th was Bucky's unit. And he hadn't been in the audience. Steve felt panic grip him. Had Bucky been captured? Or worse?

A few minutes later, Steve burst inside Phillips's tent. The colonel had arrived with Peggy after their last unsuccessful attempt to find Hydra. Now he had the miserable task of going through the paperwork to see who had survived the Azzano attack. There were a lot of names to go through.

When Steve entered the tent, Phillips's eyes narrowed. He took in Steve's ridiculous costume and wondered, not for the first time, what Brandt had been thinking. "Well, if it isn't the Star-Spangled Man with the Plan," he said.

"I need the casualty list from Azzano," Steve demanded.

Phillips raised an eyebrow. Then he pointed at the insignia on his collar stating his rank. "You don't get to give me orders, son," he said. Was this kid for real? Did he think that even with a fake title like "captain," he could order him around? But Steve wasn't going to be dissuaded.

"I don't need the whole list," he went on. "Just one name. Sergeant James Barnes. From the One Hundred and Seventh."

"You and I are going to have a conversation later that you won't enjoy," Phillips said.

"Please tell me he's alive, sir. B-A-R . . ."

"I can spell," the colonel said. "I've signed more of these condolence letters today than I would care to count."

He began to leaf through the giant pile of papers in front of him. Each paper had the name, title, and contact information of a man who had been killed in the line of duty. "The name does sound familiar," he finally said. He couldn't find the paper now, but he was sure that Barnes was one of the casualties. "I'm sorry."

Steve paled. Bucky had died fighting while Steve had been playing a clown. It wasn't fair. Turning, Steve's eyes fell on one of the maps that Phillips had tacked to the wall. It showed aerial footage of a Hydra facility. Given that the SSR had just lost men in the same vicinity, Steve figured this was where the prisoners of war were being held.

"What about the others?" he asked, turning back to the colonel. "You're planning a rescue mission, right?"

The colonel started in his seat, as though about to stand up and hit Steve for insubordination. But a glance from Peggy stopped him. Instead, he just said, "Yeah, it's called winning the war." The men from the 107th were a lost cause. Sending in a team to try to rescue them would only result in more casualties that the army couldn't afford.

"But if you know where they are—" Steve started to say, but Phillips stopped him.

"They're thirty miles behind the lines," he said. "Through some of the most heavily fortified territory in Europe. We'd lose more men than we'd save. Now if I read the posters correctly, you've got someplace to be in thirty minutes."

Phillips meant the next show, but when Steve said, "Yes, sir, I do," he meant something else.

Then, with a nod, Phillips dismissed Steve.

Turning, Steve left the tent. Phillips may not have had any intention of rescuing those men, but Steve wasn't going to sit by and do nothing. Not anymore. He'd figure out a way to get to that facility. He had to. He owed it to Bucky.

"What do you plan to do, walk to Austria?" Peggy asked.

"If that's what it takes."

"You heard the colonel. Your friend is most likely dead."

Steve would not accept this. He turned to Peggy. "You told me you thought I was meant for more than this. Did you mean that?"

"Every word," she said.

"Then you gotta let me go," he said.

Peggy thought about it. *Come on,* Steve thought. *You know I'm wasted here. You know I can do some good. Let me prove it. . . . Please let me prove it.*

"I can do more than that," she said.

Steve grabbed one of the dancing girls' USA helmets— the one with the *A* on it—and dashed off. It was time for action. Captain America was about to go behind enemy lines to rescue captured American soldiers. Steve Rogers was finally going to war.

CHAPTER 8

And so, later that night, Steve found himself inside the belly of a giant silver jet. On the bench across from him, Peggy Carter sat going over details of his seemingly impossible mission. In the cockpit, Howard Stark checked dials and instrument readings as he flew the plane farther and farther into enemy territory. He was the only pilot Peggy could find who was crazy enough to fly into enemy territory—and who didn't have to answer to Colonel Phillips. "The Hydra camp is in Krossberg," Stark was shouting over the sound of the engines. "It's up between these two mountain ranges. We should be able to drop you around the doorstep."

"Just get me as close as you can," Steve said. He would handle the rest of it himself.

Only Peggy and Stark knew what Steve was up to, and Steve shuddered at the thought of Phillips finding out. If discovered, he would surely be court-martialed and discharged from the army. But Steve wasn't about to just keep sitting around. He had seen the map. He had superstrength. And if he failed, Phillips would probably be happy to have Captain America out of his hair. Steve just wished Peggy hadn't put herself on the line for him.

"You know you two are going to be in a lot of trouble when you land," he said quietly, his voice just loud enough to carry above the whine of the engines.

"And you won't?" Peggy answered.

"Where I'm going, if anybody yells at me I can just shoot them."

"And they will undoubtedly shoot back." Peggy didn't say it, but Steve was worth the risk. After all, she'd seen him try harder than anyone else back at Camp Lehigh, even when the odds were stacked against him. And now his best friend was presumed dead and others had been captured. Of course Peggy would help.... Plus this would be the first real test of Dr. Erskine's Super-Soldier program. She had waited a long time for it.

Turning around in his seat, Stark smiled his charming smile. Unlike Steve and Peggy, he didn't seem bothered by the late-night stealth mission. In fact, he looked more confident and charming than usual.

"Well, let's hope this is good for something, Agent Carter," he said, focusing his handsome grin on Peggy. "If you're not in too much of a hurry, I thought we could stop off in Lucerne for late-night fondue."

Heat rushed to Peggy's cheeks as Steve raised an eyebrow. She grinned at the obvious jealousy on his face. "Stark's the best civilian pilot I've ever seen," she said in response to Steve's reaction. "And mad enough to brave this airspace. We're lucky to have him."

"So you two?" Steve hesitated, causing Peggy to grin even more. "Do you ... fondue?"

He was cut off by the sudden sound of gunfire. The plane lurched to the left as more guns hammered at its side. They were close to the drop zone, and Hydra didn't want them there. "This is your transponder," Peggy said, handing him the small device. "Activate it when you're ready and the signal will lead us straight to you."

Steve eyed it skeptically. "Are you sure this thing works?"

"It tested more than you, pal," Stark said from the cockpit. Pulling on his parachute, Steve opened the jump door.

The plane tilted left and then right as Stark executed evasive maneuvers. Still, the side of the plane was getting pummeled with bullets. Steve had to get out of there now before they all went down.

"Once I'm clear, turn this thing around," he said, looking at Peggy, "and get out of here!"

"You can't give me orders," Peggy shouted over the howling wind.

Steve just smiled. "Yes I can. I'm a captain!"

And then, before she could say anything else, Steve jumped, disappearing from view.

The air rushed by, whipping Steve's hair and pulling

at his clothes. Somewhere above him, he was vaguely aware that Stark had turned the plane around and was heading toward safer airspace. The guns went quiet, and Steve breathed a sigh of relief. Peggy and Stark would be okay.

He had a set count based on the plane's altitude when he jumped. *Three, two, one...* He reached it and pulled the rip cord. When the chute deployed, it slowed him so much that it felt like he was being pulled up—even though in reality he was just slowing down. When he felt steady, Steve looked down, trying to see if he could spot a clear landing place. But the only thing he could see was the flash of gunfire as bullets flew through the air.

The parachute had two steering ropes with wooden handles. They didn't help much, but they were all he had. He hauled on them, trying to angle the chute away from the enemy fire, but it was no use. Bullets ripped through the chute, and Steve began falling faster and faster. Luckily, he had made it pretty close to the ground before the shooting started, and now the forest was only about twenty feet below. Unhooking himself, Steve used his shield to brace for impact as he plummeted to the ground. Crashing through the trees as they ripped at his clothes and scratched his face, Steve landed with a thud. The gunfire stopped. The enemy must have assumed the fall had killed him. If he hadn't had Erskine's serum, they would have been right.

But as things stood, Captain America was alive and behind enemy lines, mere miles from the Hydra base.

It was time to go save some soldiers.

Moments later, Steve found himself outside the main gates to the Hydra factory. It was just where Peggy had said it would be. It was also just as heavily guarded, as she had warned. Searchlights swept from several watchtowers along the perimeter, while thick barbed wire sat atop the wall surrounding the compound. Steve could make out the main factory building, which was billowing smoke while heavily armed Hydra troopers marched back and forth across the grounds.

Steve needed a plan. Clearly he wasn't going to be able to just waltz right in there and ask for the prisoners back. The dark was suddenly illuminated by headlights as a convoy of three trucks pulled up to the gate. This was his break. As the driver of the first truck stopped to clear his entrance with the guard, Steve snuck over to the last vehicle and—making sure no one saw him—jumped inside. All he had to do was KO a couple of guards inside and hide underneath a tarp. Piece of cake. A moment later, the truck started up again and drove through the gate. Steve was in!

When he was sure that the coast was clear, Steve got out and slipped into the shadows. Now that he was inside the compound, he could make out more buildings and even more troopers. His eyes grew wide when he saw two Hydra goons leading a long line of prisoners across the compound. Steve followed them to one of the barracks. As one of the guards brought the prisoners inside, the other stood at the door on watch. With one swift move, Steve took him out using a powerful roundhouse kick. Then he silently slipped into the prison.

As soon as his eyes adjusted to the dark, Steve's mouth dropped open in terror. The barracks were something out of a nightmare. Dozens of circular cages filled the space and each one overflowed with prisoners. There had to be hundreds of them. That meant Hydra had captured more than just the 107th, Steve realized. He'd have to let Phillips know. But first, he needed to get them out.

There was a raised platform above the cages, and a guard was pacing back and forth on it. Quietly, Steve made his way up and then—*CRACK!* With a swift punch, he knocked out the guard, who then dropped off the platform and onto the cages below. The prisoners looked up, confused.

One of the men, a soldier by the name of Jones, watched as Steve stepped out of the shadows. He took in his helmet and shield. "Who are you supposed to be?" he asked.

"I'm Captain America," Steve answered, ignoring the groans that went up from the cages. He knew they had a right to doubt him. But he'd prove them wrong. He grabbed the key off the unconscious guard and raced down the line of cages, opening each one. Hordes of men spilled out, shaking their numb limbs and stretching their sore muscles.

"Are there any others?" Steve asked when everyone was out.

"The isolation ward," a British soldier named Dum Dum Dugan answered. "On the factory floor."

Steve nodded. That was where he would go next.

Leaving the others to find weapons and a way to distract the remaining guards, Steve made his way to the factory. The Hydra troopers hadn't noticed that they were under attack—yet. But they would soon, and Steve still had men to rescue. Staying in the shadows, he ducked past trooper after trooper until he finally made it to the front door. Using his red-white-and-blue shield as an offensive weapon, he smashed two Hydra guards in the face, knocking them out so he could make his way inside.

The factory floor was covered in weapons of war. There were hundreds of crates full of complete bombs and other crates with what looked like unfinished bombs. Inside even more crates, clusters of cartridges lay nestled in straw. Stepping closer, Steve noticed that the bombs and cartridges emitted a strange blue glow—just like the Super-Soldier serum. Pocketing one cartridge, he reminded himself to brief Phillips on this when—or rather, if—he got back to the base.

75

Steve then cautiously continued through the bomb-making factory, heading toward the offices at the other end of the hangar.

But, unbeknownst to Steve, the factory wasn't just another Hydra base; it was also Johann Schmidt's current headquarters. And he was watching everything Steve did over a closed-circuit camera. The Hydra leader heard a loud explosion outside and turned to look at another monitor that revealed four prisoners blasting a hole in the factory wall. As the alarm blared and guards rushed out, Schmidt turned his attention back to the image of Steve. He watched as he punched and kicked his way past dozens of guards, getting closer and closer to Schmidt's office. It was an impressive—if annoying—sight.

"Doctor," Schmidt said, turning to his lead scientist, Arnim Zola. "Prepare to evacuate."

Zola, the finest mind in Hydra (with the exception of Schmidt himself, of course), nervously eyed the camera, shifting between the action outside and the action inside the factory walls. "I'm sure our forces can handle—" he began.

"Our forces are outmatched," Schmidt snarled. "By one man," he added quietly.

Looking down at the equipment panel in front of him, Schmidt flipped a switch and a countdown clock lit up. Then he slipped out the door and down the long corridor.

Steve had just made it into the corridor when he saw the scientist retreat and heard the door to the lab close. He didn't know who the man was, but by the way he kept glancing back at the door, Steve figured something important was in there. When the other man was out of sight, Steve slipped inside and shut the door behind him.

The lab was full of files and paperwork. Specimen jars lined shelves and various monitors beeped. In the middle of the room, a large cage sat atop a rusty drain. And inside the cage, Steve saw the back of a man, who was slumped on the ground.

Hearing footsteps, the man spoke up, his voice scratchy. "Barnes, James Buchanan. Sergeant," he said.

Steve paused in midstep. It couldn't be...

"Bucky?" he said softly.

Steve raced over and crouched down in front of the cage. Bucky was inside! He was beaten and grizzled, but he was alive. With one mighty swing, Steve smashed the lock. Then he held out his hand. "It's me, Buck."

"Steve?" Bucky said, taking in his old friend's new look.

"I thought you were dead," Steve said.

"I thought you were smaller," Bucky replied as Steve hauled him to his feet and helped him out of the cage. When they were both standing, Bucky stared up at his friend, his eyes disbelieving. This wasn't the Steve he knew. This Steve was bigger, faster, and stronger than the scrawny kid Bucky grew up with in Brooklyn. And now, in a startling turn of events, Steve was about to save Bucky.

"What happened to you?" Bucky finally asked.

"I joined the army," Steve answered matter-of-factly.

Suddenly, a blast rocked the room. One of the machines on the factory floor was triggered to explode, and it sent Steve and Bucky hurtling. They would have to catch up later. Right now, they had to get out of there.

Putting an arm around Bucky, Steve began to lead

him from the room. Out of the corner of his eye, Steve spotted a map on one of the walls. He paused, noticing that it was covered in Hydra symbols that spread all across Europe. He took a mental picture of the map and then, as another explosion rocked the building, moved back into the hall with Bucky.

All around them, bombs continued to go off, shaking the foundation of the factory and making it hard to move quickly. As they made their way down the corridor, Bucky continued trying to get answers. He figured Steve must have undergone some kind of treatment or been in an experiment. There was no way he could have naturally changed into the man who stood next to him. "Did it hurt?" he asked.

"Little bit," Steve answered, dodging a piece of ceiling as it crashed to the ground.

"Is it permanent?"

"So far," Steve said.

They had reached a stairwell that led either up to a catwalk or down, back toward the factory floor. Steve started to lead them down when another series of explosions ripped through the building. A huge chunk of wall fell onto the stairs, blocking their way. It looked as if they were going to have to head up.

Dragging the still-weak Bucky, Steve got them up onto the catwalk. Outside, he heard shouts as the escaping prisoners fought against the Hydra soldiers. More bombs went off, making Steve's ears ring. When the smoke cleared, he noticed that someone was blocking their way.

"Captain America. How exciting," Johann Schmidt said, a sneer on his face. In his hand he held what looked like a titanium box. "I'm a great fan of your films," he went on. He handed the box to the man in the lab coat Steve had seen earlier. Then Schmidt moved forward. Steve took a step forward as well.

"So, Dr. Erskine managed it after all," Schmidt continued. "Not exactly an improvement, but still. Impressive."

Anger filled Steve as Schmidt spoke. With a cry of rage, he pulled back his arm and punched Schmidt as hard as he could. The Hydra leader went stumbling backward. "You've got no idea," Steve said.

A smile played over Schmidt's face and he looked

almost pleased by Steve's reaction. "Haven't I?" he asked. Then he swung. Thinking quickly, Steve threw up his mighty shield, blocking the punch. When he lowered the shield, there was a fist-size dent in it. Steve looked up, confused. A moment later, Schmidt hit him, knocking him to the ground.

"Erskine said your experiment was a failure," Steve said, trying to catch his breath. He kicked his legs, driving his feet hard into Schmidt's jaw.

Seeing his leader on the ground, the Hydra scientist raced over to the catwalk controls. His name popped into Steve's head from an intelligence file. Arnim Zola. Zola flipped a switch and the catwalk split in two, each side retracting into the walls. Steve and Schmidt were separated from each other as both men got to their feet.

When Steve looked over at the Hydra leader, his jaw dropped. It looked like Schmidt's face was on crooked. Red muscle seemed to bulge out of torn seams in Schmidt's head, as if his sinister self could no longer be contained by human skin.

"A failure?" Schmidt said. "Oh, no, Captain. I was his greatest success." Then, with an evil grin, Schmidt reached up—and pulled off his face! It had only been a mask...and underneath was a gruesome bony skull, with bloodred skin stretched tightly over it. Schmidt's eyes blazed under the heavy ridges of his eyebrows.

As Steve and Bucky gaped at the horrific sight, Schmidt let out a diabolical laugh. Then, turning, he slipped into the nearby elevator, where Arnim Zola waited. A moment later, the doors slammed shut. Schmidt had escaped, but Steve and Bucky were trapped.

Another series of explosions rocked the building, and the catwalk shuddered beneath Steve and Bucky. There was no time to worry about the Hydra leader now. They had to get out of there, or they were going to end up falling to their deaths. Before Bucky could protest, Steve picked him up and threw him across the gap between the two sides of the catwalk. He was about to follow him when—*BOOM! BOOM! BOOM!* More explosions caused the catwalk to split even wider. Steve was left stranded on one side while Bucky waited for him on the other.

"Just get out!" Steve shouted to his friend.

"Not without you!" Bucky shouted back as the roof began to collapse.

Steve looked around. The only way out was on the other side of the catwalk. He raced back as far as he could to give himself a running start and then took off. He was going to jump! He ran faster and faster. When he reached the edge, he gave himself one last push and leaped—just as the biggest bomb went off.

Bucky watched in horror as Steve disappeared into the flames.

CHAPTER 9

olonel Phillips sat in front of his typewriter, his fingers hesitating over the keys. Taking a deep breath, he continued his note: *Senator Brandt. Regret to report Cpt. Steven Rogers KIA.* He stopped typing as Peggy Carter came to the door. She looked tired and sad. In her hand, she held aerial photographs of the destroyed Hydra camp. "No sign of activity," she reported.

Phillips stared at her, his expression cold. She had

disobeyed direct orders and helped Steve on his ill-fated mission. While Phillips had never really liked Steve, he didn't think the kid should have been put in a situation like that. He wasn't equipped to handle it—even if he had a "captain" before his name.

"We can't touch Stark," Phillips said after a tense moment of silence. "He's rich, and he's the army's number one weapons contractor. *You* are neither."

Peggy nodded. She had expected that reaction. And frankly, she didn't care. Not anymore. Not with Steve dead. "You'll have my resignation in the morning," she said. She paused, as if not sure whether to go on. "With respect, sir, I don't regret my actions. And I doubt Captain Rogers did, either."

"What makes you think I give a damn about your opinions? I took a chance on you, Agent Carter," Phillips said, untouched by her words. "Now America's golden boy—and a lot of other men—are dead. Because you had a *crush*."

"It wasn't that," she said. "It was faith." But Colonel Phillips didn't hear her because of a rising commotion outside. Soldiers were running by, shouting to one another excitedly. Walking to the window, Peggy and Phillips looked out. The gates to the camp were opening. And beyond them—battered and bruised but very much alive—was Captain America.

Steve and Bucky walked slowly up the road, leading the squad of rescued soldiers back to their Italian home. A ragtag group of vehicles followed farther behind, carrying the wounded and weak.

Once inside the base, Steve pushed through the growing crowd and made his way over to Phillips and Peggy. "Colonel," he said, his tone weary, "some of these men need medical attention." Phillips nodded and Steve went on. "I'd like to surrender myself for disciplinary action."

The colonel looked at Steve, then at the soldiers stumbling into the camp, and then back at Steve. Despite the bruises and scratches all over his body, Steve's eyes were alert. The events at the factory had changed him. He wasn't the same man who had gone beyond enemy lines. He had faced real danger—and survived.

"That won't be necessary," Phillips finally said.

"Yes, sir," Steve said.

Phillips turned to Peggy. "Faith, huh?"

Then he walked away, leaving Steve openmouthed with shock. He had finally proven himself to the toughest man he knew. Turning, his eyes met Peggy's. There was a jolt of electricity, and Steve felt his heart begin to race. There was so much he wanted to say to her. But she beat him to it. "You're late," she stated.

He smiled. That was probably the closest he was going to get to a "welcome home" from Peggy. But he'd take it. "Couldn't call my ride," he said, teasing her.

Before he could say more, soldiers crowded around him, clapping him on the back and congratulating him. Peggy stayed right with him. Steve couldn't keep the smile from his face. For the first time since he'd donned the Captain America costume, he truly felt like a hero. And it felt good.

A few days later, Steve attended a briefing at the London headquarters of the SSR. A newspaper lay on one of the tables. Its headline read: CAPTAIN AMERICA TO RECEIVE MEDAL OF VALOR.

However, Steve had no interest in attending the ceremony. Medals didn't matter to him. What mattered was winning the war. As Peggy and Stark looked on, Steve sketched out the locations of the Hydra bases he had seen back in Schmidt's office.

"One here in Poland, one on the Baltic, and the sixth one was...about...thirty, forty miles west of the Maginot Line," he said, adding the last three. Then, looking over at Peggy and Stark, he added, "I just got a quick look."

Peggy smiled. Since he had returned from the Hydra camp, things had changed between them. They both felt a spark lying just below the surface, ready to ignite. "Nobody's perfect," she said, her eyes twinkling.

Just then, Colonel Phillips entered. Walking over, he glanced at the map on the table and then at the blue cartridge Steve had taken from the Hydra factory. "You figure out what this is yet?" Phillips asked.

Howard Stark had suffered through Steve and Peggy's flirting for far too long. Eager for a diversion, he answered, "The most powerful explosive known to man, according to Rogers." There was a hint of bitterness in Stark's voice. He prided himself on inventing the most powerful things. He didn't like it that he'd been beaten to the punch. Taking out a pair of tweezers, he gingerly picked up the cartridge.

"Either Schmidt's darn near rewritten the laws of physics," he went on, "or this isn't from—" He couldn't say it out loud. It seemed impossible that Schmidt's delusional belief in gods and other worlds could have any basis in fact. He shook his head. "I can *say* that if they've got enough of it, this war isn't going the way anyone thinks it is."

The room fell silent as Stark's words sank in. They were at a critical point in the war. If this cartridge was just one of many, then the results would be worldwide annihilation—and Hydra domination.

Walking over to the map, Phillips began tracing the various *x*'s that marked the Hydra camps. "Then we'd better take it away from them," he finally said. "These are the weapons factories we're talking about?"

Steve put down his pencil and shook his head. "Not all of them," he answered. "Bucky—I mean Sergeant Barnes—said Hydra shipped all the parts to another facility that isn't on this map."

Bucky overheard a lot while he'd been kept in the

cage in Hydra's science lab. He filled Steve in on as much as he could remember during the trek back from the factory. This piece of information was the most important of all.

The room fell silent again as they all processed the news that there were more bombs out there. Bombs of otherworldly power. They needed to get their hands on them before Schmidt had the chance to use them. And while they didn't know where the majority of the bombs were being shipped, thanks to Steve's map they *did* know where the other Hydra bases were. Maybe destroying them would put Schmidt on edge and give SSR the advantage.

"Agent Carter," Colonel Phillips said. "Coordinate with MI6. I want every Allied eyeball looking for that main Hydra base."

"What about us?"

"We are going to light a fire under Johann Schmidt's ass," Colonel Phillips said. Turning to face Steve, he smiled. "What do you say, Rogers? It's your map. Think you can wipe Hydra off of it?"

Steve returned the smile. There was nothing he

would like to do more. And he had the perfect team in mind to help him....

The Whip and Fiddle was a local London pub that served cold drinks, warm food, and good cheer. That night, it was full of the soldiers Steve had helped rescue from the Hydra factory. Making his way through the crowd, Steve found Bucky in the back, leaning against a barstool. Five other men—Falsworth, Jones, Dernier, Morita, and Dugan—stood a bit to the side. Since rescuing them, these men had become Steve's friends and, he hoped, they'd now become his teammates.

"Let me get this straight," Dum Dum Dugan said after Steve explained the mission. "We barely got out of there alive, and you want us to go back?"

"Pretty much," Steve answered, nodding.

Dugan shrugged. "Sounds rather...fun, actually," he said. The other four nodded in agreement, and Steve tried not to laugh. That had been easier than he expected. Now he had the rest of the night to have a good time before they set out in the morning.

Turning, he joined Bucky at the bar. "What about

you?" Steve asked when they were alone. "You ready to follow Captain America into the jaws of death?"

To Steve's surprise, Bucky shook his head. "No," he answered, and Steve's mouth dropped open. Then Bucky added, "That little guy from Brooklyn—the kid in the alley who couldn't stay down, and wouldn't take no for an answer? I'm following him."

Steve smiled at his old friend.

"You're keeping the outfit, right?" Bucky asked.

Steve nodded. "It's kind of growing on me."

They were still talking about strategy and the mission when Steve looked up and saw Peggy making her way through the crowd. She had traded her usual uniform for a red dress and looked beautiful. Noticing that his friend was distracted, Bucky turned and saw Peggy. He smiled. Not bad.

"Captain," she said.

"Agent Carter."

Bucky stood. "Ma'am."

Joining them, Peggy informed Steve that he had an early morning meeting with Stark. Apparently, the inventor had been working day and night to create some new equipment and needed Steve to come by and try it out. Then she noticed Falsworth and Jones were standing in the middle of the room, singing at the top of their lungs. Dernier and Morita looked on, laughing as the two men tried to pull a couple of girls in for a dance.

"I see your crack top squad is prepping for duty," she observed.

Bucky gave Peggy one of his trademark grins. The one that had caused plenty of Brooklyn girls to go weak at the knees. "You don't like music?" he asked playfully.

"I do, actually," Peggy answered, looking not at Bucky but at Steve. "I may even, when this is all over, go dancing."

The music grew louder, but it seemed that Peggy and Steve couldn't hear it. They just continued to look at each other, as though having a silent conversation. Growing tired of it, Bucky held out a hand and said, "Then what are you waiting for?"

Never looking away from Steve, Peggy said, "The right partner." Then she executed a turn in her stunning dress and left them there with Dugan's band of drunken maniacs.

Bucky groaned. "I'm invisible!" he cried. Then a realization struck him and he laughed. "I'm turning into you. It's a horrible dream."

Steve gave him a wicked smile. "Don't take it so hard," he said teasingly. "Maybe she's got a friend."

As Bucky stormed off, Steve just stood there with a smile on his face. True, he was about to go on a dangerous mission. But things suddenly felt really good. He had his best friend back, a great team to rely on, and maybe, just maybe, a future with Peggy. For the first time in a long while, things were beginning to look up.

CHAPTER 10

The next morning, Steve reported to Stark's office as requested. But when he got there, Stark had not yet arrived. A young blond woman sitting behind a desk informed Steve that the inventor would be there in a minute. Then she introduced herself as Private Lorraine.

"The women of America owe you their thanks," she said, getting up and walking over to Steve. "And seeing as they're not here..." Before Steve knew what was happening, Private Lorraine leaned in, and they were kissing.

Just then, Peggy entered the office, and the look on her face could have turned a man to stone. "Captain," she said in a voice that froze him where he stood. "We're ready for you. If you're not otherwise occupied."

Turning, she stalked out the door. Steve followed, hot on her heels.

"Agent Carter!" he called. "Peggy! Wait a second!"

"Looks like finding a partner wasn't that hard after all," she said.

"That's not what you thought it was," Steve said.

"I don't think anything, Captain," she said. "Not one thing. Always wanted to be a soldier, and now you are. Just like all the rest."

It wasn't right! But he couldn't convince her. "Well, what about you and Stark?" he said. "How do I know you two haven't been...fondue-ing?"

She looked at him, still angry, but now with something like pity in her expression, too. "You still don't know a bloody thing about women," she said.

That was when Howard Stark finally showed up. Apparently he'd overheard some of the conversation, because he said, "Fondue's just cheese and bread, my friend."

"Really? I didn't think . . ."

"Nor should you, pal," Stark said. "The minute you think you know what's going on in a woman's head, your goose is well and truly cooked. Me, I concentrate on work. Which, at the moment, is about making sure you and your men do not get killed."

After giving Private Lorraine a grin, he led Steve down to his lab, where technicians were busy unwrapping various pieces of equipment. Others were installing futuristic machines like those Steve had seen back at the World Exhibition of Tomorrow. Peggy stood to one side, her arms crossed.

Ignoring everyone else, Stark walked over to a slightly-less-cluttered section of the lab. Lying on a table was what looked like a bodysuit. Steve cocked his head. What on earth was it?

"Steel micromesh for the sleeves," Stark explained,

pointing to the suit's arms. "Titanium panels for your more vulnerable parts. Chest plates...and such."

Steve's eyes grew wide as Stark moved down the table and picked up a gray-colored material. He was getting his very own, state-of-the-art combat suit. "Carbon polymer," Stark went on. "It's flexible, insulated, fire-resistant, and ought to hold its own against your average German bayonet. Although Hydra's not going to attack you with a pocketknife."

And that's when Stark guided Steve over to another table and presented him with the biggest surprise of all. "I hear you're, uh...kind of attached," he said, pointing.

On the table was an array of shields, in various stages of construction. Some of them had gadgets on them, one had lights, and another looked like it had been painted with camouflage.

"It's handier than you might think," Steve said.

"I took the liberty of coming up with some options," Stark said, and started pointing out different features of different shields. Steve's attention, however, went imme-diately to a plain silver one lying at the end of the table partially covered with a tarp.

It didn't have any gadgets or lights or hidden compart-ments. Instead, it was lightweight, balanced, and almost indestructible. It was the perfect offensive and defensive symbol of the United States of America, and it would become Captain America's most trusted and well-known weapon. Cautiously, Steve reached out and ran a hand across the shield's smooth surface. Then he gave it a tap, and it rang like a bell.

"What about this one?" he asked.

"No, that's just a prototype."

"What's it made of?"

"Vibranium," Stark informed them. "A hundred times stronger than steel and one-third the weight." Picking it up, Steve slid the shield onto his arm as Stark continued. "It's completely vibration absorbent. Should make a bullet feel like a cotton ball."

Steve smiled. This was the best thing he'd ever seen, if it was true. "Then how come it's not standard issue?"

"That's the rarest metal on Earth. What you're holding there, that's all we've got."

"Are you quite finished, Mr. Stark?" Peggy asked. "I'm sure the captain has some unfinished business."

Steve hefted the shield. He was already loving how light and strong it felt. He turned to Peggy and asked, "What do you think?"

In answer, she picked up a gun from a nearby lab table. She leveled it at him and fired four times. Steve ducked behind the shield, bracing himself for the impact of the bullets—but one after another, they hit the shield and plunked harmlessly to the ground. He barely felt the impacts.

"Yes, I think it works," she said. Then she stalked out of the room.

Steve gulped. He had some serious explaining to do. Howard Stark tried to hide a grin.

But it would have to wait. Right now, he had to go after Hydra. Lucky for him, he seemed to have an excellent new shield to make the mission a little easier. He prodded the four flattened slugs on the lab floor. This vibranium was pretty amazing. Steve looked over at Stark, who just shrugged.

Steve hoped that Peggy would forgive him by the time he came back.

CHAPTER 11

For the next few months, Captain America and his ragtag unit of Howling Commandos traveled all over Europe, chasing down and destroying as many Hydra bases as they could find.

First, they headed to France. This was one of the weaker Hydra stations, and in no time, the team took it over. Back at their headquarters, Peggy replaced one of the x's with an SSR flag.

Then they headed to Poland, where Bucky took

out the guard at the front gate so the team could enter. As the others streamed past them, he and Steve traded knowing smiles. It was just like being back in Brooklyn—only slightly more dangerous. Another SSR flag was pinned on the map.

Next up was a base in Czechoslovakia. Signaling for the others to wait, Captain America made his way inside by himself. Ducking and weaving past the Hydra troopers, he found the collection of bombs. He quickly placed a detonator among them and then grabbed one of the trooper's bikes, jumped on it, and raced away. He barely managed to crash through a factory window before the place exploded behind him. Another base destroyed.

The rest of the team was having fun taking revenge against the organization that had held them prisoner. In Greece, Dernier set another explosive charge and—*BOOM!*—the place blew to bits. Pinned down in Germany, Morita shouted coordinates to Jones over a handheld radio. Jones quickly fired his weapon while at the same time Falsworth threw a grenade. The base exploded. Another Hydra camp down.

The team's wave of destruction did not go unnoticed. Johann Schmidt had taken refuge in a secret Greek camp, one of the few remaining Hydra strongholds. Standing in front of his troop leaders, Schmidt, now known to his followers as the Red Skull, raged on. "We are close to an offensive that will shake the planet," he said angrily. "Yet we are continually delayed because you can't outwit a clown dressed in a flag!"

This was unacceptable. Captain America and his Howling Commandos needed to be taken out. Fast. For the first time since the attacks began, the Red Skull's evil smile returned. He had come up with a good idea. An idea that would take care of Captain America—once and for all.

Unaware of the Red Skull's plans, Cap, Bucky, and the rest of the team gathered on a plateau high above a Russian valley. The sun was not up yet, and the wind was cold as it whipped around them.

Steve was nervous. There had been no base in this

area marked on the map. Which meant it was either a trap or a huge find. Using one of the Hydra code transceivers they'd stolen from a captured base, they had intercepted a transmission claiming that a large Hydra train was on the move through a nearby Alpine pass and that Hydra's top scientist was on board. Steve had made the decision to act. It was risky to go into unknown territory, but this might be the chance they needed to finish off Hydra once and for all.

As Jones listened to another transmission, Dugan and Falsworth kept a lookout on the valley below. Meanwhile, Cap, Bucky, and Dernier moved closer to the edge.

"The train engineer just radioed ahead," Jones called out. "Hydra gave him permission to open the throttle. Wherever their base is, he's trying to make it there by dawn." He paused and then added, "With their biggest shipment yet."

Just then, a train whistle blew, piercing the silence of the night. Looking through his binoculars, Dugan saw a large, futuristic-looking train racing down the tracks. Turning, he nodded at Steve. It was time.

"Remember when I made you ride the Cyclone on Coney Island?" Bucky asked Steve.

"Yeah, and I threw up."

"This isn't payback, is it?"

"Now why would I do that?"

Jones called out again. "Dr. Zola is on this train. Wherever he's going, they must need him bad."

"We've only got about a ten-second window," Steve said. "You miss that window...we're bugs on a windshield."

Quickly, Dernier helped Cap, Bucky, and Jones strap into harnesses. Then he snapped three hooks onto a long cable that stretched out over the pass. This was how they were going to get on the train. But they had to time it just right. If they didn't, they'd either be crushed by the train—or by the opposite wall of the valley.

The train whistle blew again and Captain America nodded at his men. "Mind the gap," Falsworth said.

Now! Together, they pushed off, zipping down toward the oncoming train. For a moment, it looked as if they were going to miss, but then with a *THUD!* they landed on the slick roof. Unhooking themselves, they let the cable fly away. They didn't want to leave any evidence of their presence.

As planned, Jones headed toward the engine of the train. His mission was to somehow stop the train so the rest of the team would have enough time to get down there. Steve and Bucky, meanwhile, were going after the explosives.

Jumping down into the train, the squad found themselves in the first car. It was empty. Moving into the next car, they exchanged looks. It was empty, too. This didn't seem right. Cautiously, they entered the next car. Unlike the others, this car was pitch-dark. And eerily quiet. Steve couldn't even hear the sound of the rushing wind outside. Then, *WHAM!* Behind them, a steel plate dropped down, blocking the back door.

A moment later, the lights flickered on. It was a trap! Standing in front of them was the largest Hydra trooper Steve had ever seen. The monster of a man was easily over six and a half feet tall, and instead of arms, he had two huge, robotic cannons attached to his shoulders. It was the perfect plan. The Red Skull had lured Captain America here so that this *thing* could kill him.

Steve shook his head in revolt. He and his men had come too far to let that happen. Pulling out his gun, Cap opened fire, but the bullets just zinged harmlessly off the trooper's armor. Then, as Steve watched in horror, the trooper raised one of his cannon "arms," aimed, and fired. *BLAM!* A blue energy pulse sent Steve flying into the sidewall of the train, knocking the breath out of him.

He recovered and used the ceiling racks to swing the length of the train car in a single motion, driving both feet into the Hydra trooper and knocking him down. Then a blow from Steve's shield kept him down.

But Bucky was trapped in the other car, pinned down by another Hydra soldier. He was out of ammunition. Steve rushed to the door and caught Bucky's eye through the window. He opened the door and tossed Bucky his own pistol, then dove into the car so his shield provided cover for Bucky to return fire. Bucky put the Hydra trooper down.

They looked at each other. "I had him on the ropes," Bucky said.

Steve nodded. "I know you did."

Then another burst of blue energy seared through the car, blasting a huge hole in one wall. Air rushed by and they could see down to the distant floor of the icy canyon. The trooper with the cannons was back! Steve dropped his shield as he dove out of the way. Bucky picked it up and advanced as the trooper recharged. He aimed at Bucky. Another burst came from the cannon and blasted Bucky out through the hole! He dropped the shield and caught onto one rung of a ladder on the outside of the car. The valley walls rushed by as the train continued to speed on. Struggling to his feet, Captain America held up his shield and started to advance on the giant trooper. Once again, the Hydra agent held up one of his cannon arms. The weapon hummed as the blue energy filled it and the trooper leveled it out—aiming right for the star on Steve's chest.

The blue energy burst out of the cannon in a steady stream. But Cap lifted his shield just in the nick of time, and the energy hit it instead of him. With determined steps, Captain America pushed against the stream of energy, getting closer and closer to the trooper. Then, with one last mighty shove, he pushed the shield out in front of him, sending all the blue energy right back at the Hydra agent, blasting him through into the other car. This time he was down for good.

There was no time to celebrate. Steve clambered out through the hole. "Bucky!" he screamed over the roaring wind. "Hang on!"

But the ladder was giving way, and Steve was too far to reach! Steve tried to get closer. "Grab my hand!" he shouted, and reached...

And the rung broke free. "No!" Steve cried out, lunging for his friend, but he couldn't save him. Bucky fell, disappearing into the windswept depths of the canyon.

Steve clung to the outside of the car, watching, unable to believe what he'd seen. Bucky, his oldest friend... the one he'd always looked up to...

He was gone.

Steve pulled himself back inside the car. The rest of the Howling Commandos had finished their sweep, and Jones was there, prodding Arnim Zola in front of him with the barrel of his gun. They had captured Hydra's main scientific mind, and Hydra's plan to trap and destroy Captain America and his Howling Commandos had failed.

The mission was a success...but with Bucky gone, it didn't feel that way.

CHAPTER 12

Captain America and his team made their way back to London headquarters. Phillips had ordered them to bring the scientist Zola right to him. It was time to get answers.

It didn't take long to break the weaselly man. He wanted to talk because all crazy people wanted to talk. Colonel Phillips brought him a good meal, which in his experience usually got people talking. Zola refused the steak because he was a vegetarian. So Phillips ate while he asked questions. Eventually they got down to business, when Phillips handed Zola an encrypted note he'd sent to Washington. "'Given the valuable information he has provided, and in exchange for his full cooperation, Dr. Zola is being remanded to Switzerland,'" Zola read.

"Of course it was encoded. You guys haven't broken those codes, have you? That would be awkward."

"He will know this is a lie," Zola said.

"He's going to kill you anyway, Doc. You're a liability. You know more about Schmidt than anyone. And the last guy you cost us was Captain Rogers's closest friend. So I wouldn't count on the very best of protection. It's you . . . or Schmidt."

He watched Zola process this and understand he had no other option than to give Phillips what he wanted.

"Schmidt believes he walks in the footsteps of gods," Zola said. "Only the entire world will satisfy him."

"You do realize that's nuts, don't you?"

"Of course. The sanity of the plan is of no consequence."

"And why is that?"

"Because he can do it," Zola said.

Phillips thought about this while he finished the steak. It was hard to get a good steak in these parts. He set down his knife and fork. Schmidt was nuts, that much they knew. But the entire world? What did Zola mean by that? Phillips needed some more specific answers. "What's his target?" the colonel asked.

"Everywhere," Zola said. He had a funny little smile on his face.

After a few more hours of interrogation, Phillips had all the information he was going to get. He met with Peggy and ran through what he had learned. Then he called the others into the conference room. When everyone was settled, he began. "Johann Schmidt belongs in the bughouse," he said. "He thinks he's a god, and he's going to blow up half the world to prove it."

Peggy stood up and walked over to a map of the world. "Starting with the United States." The room grew silent as everyone processed the news. Peggy went on. "Schmidt's working with powers beyond our capabilities. He gets across the Atlantic, he'll wipe out the entire Eastern Seaboard in an hour." As she spoke, she looked directly at Steve. Since he had returned from his latest mission, he had been withdrawn and quiet. They did not have the opportunity to talk about what had happened with Private Lorraine, and now it seemed they might never have the chance. A shiver of fear ran through her as she thought about what this latest intel meant for Steve—and for her.

As Peggy spoke, everyone in the room turned and looked at the map, their eyes focusing on New York City. They were each thinking the same thing. The United States was completely defenseless against an attack of that magnitude. The majority of soldiers had been deployed to Europe or the Pacific. Schmidt was heading across the Atlantic—they had to act fast.

"How much time have we got?" Dernier asked.

Phillips looked grave. "According to my new best friend, twenty-four hours."

No one said anything for a moment. They had just returned from fighting Hydra and were tired, having been pushed to their limits. But they couldn't sit around and do nothing.

"Where is the Red Skull now?" Steve asked, standing up.

"Hydra's last base is here, in the Alps," Phillips said, pointing to the map. Then he traced his finger down as he added, "Five hundred feet below the surface."

Steve nodded. This wasn't going to be easy. But they could do it. They *had* to do it. Looking at the rest of his team, he saw that they had the same determination in their eyes that he probably did.

Captain America and the Howling Commandos were heading to the Alps.

CHAPTER 13

Cap and his team worked quickly to prepare for their next—and hopefully last—mission. Stark outfitted them with equipment capable of taking out Hydra's defenses and of protecting them from enemy fire. While Steve gave the rest of the team a few hours off to relax and recharge, Peggy and Phillips briefed him on the layout of the base and the surrounding landscape. He would be taking the lead in the attack. The others would follow him once he was in, providing backup and, if necessary, an escape route. The part of the base that was aboveground would be well guarded, but it would still be easy for Captain America to sneak in. The tricky part would be finding the Red Skull amid the labyrinthine corridors and rooms deep below the surface. The SSR didn't have specific information on where the Hydra leader would be holing up inside. Steve would be going in blind.

But he wasn't worried. In fact, he had a plan that he hadn't shared with Peggy or Phillips. If everything went as he suspected it would, the Red Skull would come to him....

Soon, everything was in place. The team, including Peggy and Phillips, took a plane to a designated spot a few dozen miles from the base. Their hope was to land undetected, which would give Steve a head start. After that, it was up to him.

A few hours after landing, Captain America raced his motorcycle through the dense forest near the Hydra base. His team was behind him, getting ready for their part, and Steve was running on pure adrenaline. He was finally going to take the Red Skull down and make the evil man pay for all the death and destruction he had been responsible for. Whatever happened today, Captain America had only one goal—to face the Red Skull alone.

He was so focused on Schmidt that he didn't notice when his bike unwittingly tripped a wire lying across the small road. Nearby, in a secret Hydra outpost, a warning light blinked. Seeing it, two Hydra guards leaped onto their bikes and headed toward the road. Soon, they had caught up to Steve.

The sound of roaring engines caused Cap to turn as the Hydra troopers drove onto the road. They were just a few feet behind him, and gaining fast. Revving his engine, Captain America shot forward. But the sentries were too close; they gained on him. Before he could maneuver away, one of them jerked his handlebars to the left, sideswiping Cap's bike. The motorcycle wobbled, but Steve managed to steady it. Then he quickly jerked his wheel to the right, causing him to career into the trooper. There was the sound of metal crunching as the bike frames crashed into each other.

Captain America needed to get rid of this trooper.

Looking up ahead, he smiled. It seemed he'd just found a way. Gunning his engine, he hunched low over the handlebars and sped forward, the trooper staying right behind him. Then, at the last moment, Cap dropped his bike into a slide—ducking below a low-hanging branch. The trooper didn't have time to react and—*WHACK!*—he hit the branch head-on. The Hydra agent went flying, his bike exploding in the fiery crash.

There was no time to celebrate taking down the guard. Gunshots rang out as the other trooper pulled his pistol and began firing. Cap ducked and wove his bike down the road, trying to stay out of the way of the flying bullets. But he couldn't keep it up forever. Thinking quickly, he slammed on his brakes, the tires screeching on the pavement. In moments, the trooper caught up with him. When he did, Cap grabbed the handlebars of the other bike. Using all his superstrength, he clung tightly as the trooper swerved back and forth across the road. Steve stuck like glue. Seeing a huge pine tree ahead, Steve jerked the sentry's bike toward it. Just before they were about to crash, Steve turned at the last possible second, saving himself from certain death. But the Hydra agent couldn't get away. His bike slammed into the pine and exploded.

Steve smiled. Two down, a few more to go. It was time to get inside the Hydra base.

The Hydra base was built into the side of a mountain in the Alps, its outside buildings protected by a large wall topped with barbed wire. Alarms were already sounding as Captain America approached, but he didn't care. This was all part of his plan. The plan he hadn't told Peggy or Phillips about. But he did tell the Howling Commandos about it, and hopefully they were at the ready.

When he was about twenty feet away from the wall, Cap gunned his bike's engine. A few feet later, he pulled back on the handlebars. As the engine groaned under the effort, he jumped the bike up and over the wall. He landed with a thud safely on the other side.

Hydra troopers immediately opened fire as Steve tore across the compound. With lightning-quick reflexes, he stayed ahead of the bullets and laid the bike down in an expert slide, leaping free to join the fray. He fought off as many Hydra troopers as he could, but there were just too many of them. They surrounded him, energy weapons leveled.

Captain America had been captured.

A few minutes later, Captain America found himself inside Johann Schmidt's office. It was dark and oppressive. On one wall, a large picture of Schmidt, with his red skull showing in all its hideous glory, was displayed. Steve didn't know whether it was supposed to serve as a warning to those who entered, or whether Schmidt was so crazy he just liked to look at his disfigured face.

The Red Skull circled him, with a sneer. "Arrogance may not be a uniquely American trait," he said, "but I must say you do it better than anyone. Still, there are limits to what even you can do, Captain. Or did Erskine tell you otherwise?"

"He told me you were insane," Steve said.

"Ah," Schmidt said. "He resented my genius, and tried to deny me what was rightfully mine. But he gave you everything. So. What made you so special?"

"Nothing," Steve said. "I'm just a kid from Brooklyn." The Red Skull hit him, and he went down.

Struggling, he turned and tried to kick Schmidt, but Steve was in an awkward position and the kick went wide. Grabbing Cap's foot, the Hydra leader swung Captain America into a wall, instantly knocking the wind out of him. But Captain America wasn't ready to give up yet.

"I can do this all day," Steve said, breathing heavily. Just like he'd said to the bully back in the Brooklyn alley. He had strength and power now, but he had always had will and determination. That was more important. That's what Dr. Erskine had meant when, with his dying breath, he had tapped on Steve's chest. Heart mattered the most.

"I believe you can," the Red Skull replied. He pulled out his pistol and aimed it at Steve's head, his hand steady. "But I am on a tight schedule."

Captain America didn't look scared or upset. In fact, he looked...happy?

"So am I," he said just as the office window behind him shattered. Falsworth and the rest of the Howling

Commandos crashed into the room, swinging from ropes and firing their weapons. Using the distraction to his advantage, Captain America rose to his feet and barreled into the Red Skull. The Hydra leader went flying into the far wall, leaving a human-size dent in it. Meanwhile, explosions rocked the base above.

Rage filled Schmidt's red face, turning it even redder. Reaching out, he gave Captain America a one-two punch that sent him flying backward. As Cap tried to recover, Schmidt raced across the room and grabbed a titanium box. It was the same one that Steve had seen back when he had rescued Bucky. Whatever was inside must be important to Schmidt, he thought. Steve planned on taking it from the Hydra leader before destroying him.

As Steve watched, Schmidt bolted from the room. The rest of Steve's team had taken care of the Hydra troopers who had tried to fight them and were now cleaning up the mess. Steve picked up his shield and made sure the area was secure...but he had to go after Schmidt! At the same moment, more guards entered and fired their weapons. All of them shouted, "Hail

Hydra!" One went on, "Cut off one head, two more shall rise—"

Just then, a *BLAM!* finished the trooper's sentence as he fell to the ground. Colonel Phillips strode through the base, machine gun in hand, and addressed the Howling Commandos. "Then let's go find two more," he said. Confident that the colonel and the Howling Commandos could handle the rest of the Hydra troopers, Steve turned and raced down the corridor.

Captain America was going after the Red Skull.

CHAPTER 14

The underground base was full of corridors that twisted and turned, making it easy to get lost. Turning a corner, Captain America saw the Red Skull up ahead, the box still clutched tightly in his hand. He put on a burst of speed. Hearing footsteps, the Red Skull turned and pulled out a gun. It looked a lot like the one Steve had seen on the train. As he watched, it filled with blue energy and the blast came straight at him. Quickly, Cap raised his vibranium shield, and the blue energy splashed against it in a brilliant flash of light. Amazing, Steve thought. He'd seen men completely disintegrated by those weapons, and their impact on the shield wasn't any harder than a raindrop.

He'd lost a step on Schmidt, though, and when Steve started running again, Schmidt was already around a bend in the corridor. Steve heard the unmistakable grinding of a heavy mechanical blast door starting to close. There was no way Captain America was going to let the Red Skull get away. Not when he was this close to taking down the Hydra leader. Pulling his arm back, he flung the shield so it glanced off the wall. With any luck, he'd nail Schmidt on his way through the door....

THUNK! That was not the sound of the shield hitting a Hydra Super-Soldier. More like the sound a shield might make when it jammed itself into the narrowing gap between two sides of a heavy blast door.

Standing up on the other side, Steve looked around. There was nowhere to go but straight ahead. He quickly began running down the corridor only to come to a screeching halt. Standing in front of him, holding two weapons that looked like huge flamethrowers, stood a

Hydra trooper. The trooper had a tank, filled to the top with the powerful and deadly blue substance, strapped to his back. Steve gulped. This wasn't good.

Raising the twin guns, the trooper pulled a trigger. On his back, the tank gurgled and whined as it sent fiery blue energy through the tubes and into the guns. Cap lifted his hand reflexively, thinking his shield was still on his forearm. But then he remembered. It was jammed in the blast door around the bend ahead, thanks to his long-range shot at the Red Skull. He was completely defenseless. Steve pressed himself into a nearby recessed doorway as the trooper blasted the hall with a flaming geyser. Cap held his spot, feeling enough heat that he was surprised he didn't just go up like a Roman candle. He had a feeling superstrength wasn't going to make him fireproof.

The flame winked out. If the Hydra trooper's weapon was like most flamethrowers, he had to interrupt the fire every so often or its barrels would melt. Steve glanced out into the hall. Everything that wasn't metal was on fire. Seeing Steve, the trooper fired up the flamethrowers again. *Uh-oh,* Steve thought. He started to duck back into the doorway again, hoping he could time a jump out to disable the Hydra trooper the next time he let the flames go out.

As he moved, he heard a sharp burst of gunfire. He hit the ground as the Hydra trooper's canister went up in a blue flare and he went down face-first onto the scorched steel floor.

When the smoke from the blast cleared, there was Peggy Carter coming out of a side corridor.

"You're late," Steve said, smiling at her. He had never been so happy to see anyone in his life. Peggy smiled back at him, her eyes warm. With a wave of thanks, Captain America took off after the Red Skull.

When he got to the blast door, he ducked under his shield and then jerked it out of the gap. The door finished grinding its way closed. Steve spun around, not knowing what to expect. He found himself inside a giant hangar built deep into the mountain. A rumbling filled the air. As Steve watched, a gigantic plane rolled past. But this was no normal plane. It was a design he'd never seen before: a flying wing, basically. Like a giant steel arrowhead, at least four times the size of the biggest US Army plane. It had four giant turbo propeller engines and it bristled with gun turrets. Looking around, Steve noticed that there were five more just like it! These must be the planes that Schmidt was going to use to attack the United States. *They're big enough to carry the blue bombs and thousands of Hydra troopers,* he realized.

Looking back at the plane that was making its way down the hangar, Steve saw Schmidt sitting in the cockpit. The Hydra leader turned and smiled. Steve couldn't stop him now. The plane began moving faster and faster. At the other end of the hangar, giant doors began to open, letting in the glare of sunlight. This wasn't just a hangar—it was a runway!

Captain America started sprinting, but it was no use. The Red Skull was too far ahead. Steve was fast, but not as fast as a giant plane. His fists pumped at his sides as he tried harder and harder to pick up speed. He was just about to give up when the sound of a car engine came from right next to him. Looking over, Steve saw Colonel Phillips sitting behind the wheel of Schmidt's custom Hydra roadster. Peggy was in the backseat.

Quickly, Steve leaped into the car as Phillips stepped on the gas, sending them shooting forward. In moments, they had caught up with the plane. The car shuddered as Phillips pulled it up next to the plane's large back tire. The wheel was attached to long metal landing gear that extended up to the inside of the plane itself.

Captain America stood. He was glad the car was a convertible. It would have been harder to get onto the landing gear through the window. He was about to make the jump, when Peggy let out a shout. "Wait!" she cried. Then, before Steve knew what was happening, she pulled him into a kiss. For a moment, Steve forgot about Schmidt. He forgot about Hydra and the pending attack. For once in his life, Steve Rogers got the girl. Reluctantly, he pulled away. He had to go. Hopefully, he'd return from this mission and ask Peggy to a dance.

"Go get him!" Colonel Phillips shouted over the sound of the plane's engines. "I'm not kissing you!"

Steve cracked a smile. After one last look at Peggy, he turned and jumped onto the wheel—just as the plane burst out of the tunnel. Behind him, Steve saw Phillips slam on the brakes and drag the car into a sideways drift. He breathed a sigh of relief when the car stopped just on the edge of a long drop down the mountain. They were okay. Steve's own situation was a little more tricky. The jet was flying over a huge gorge, and Steve was losing his grip. If he fell now, there was no way he would survive.

Just then, the plane's landing gear groaned and slowly started to retract. He let out a huge breath. That had been *way* too close for comfort.

Steve's relief was short-lived. As he let go of the landing gear, he found himself looking at a huge flight deck within the belly of the giant plane. Eight fighter jets were armed and ready, their noses aimed toward the back hatch of the plane.

He'd been right! This was one of the planes that were going to attack the United States! And there were five more back inside the hangar—unless Phillips and the team had managed to stop them from taking off. Captain America had to find the Red Skull—now.

Unfortunately, that was going to be a bit difficult. As he watched, the eight pilots who belonged to those fighter jets ran down from the bridge above. All of them had guns trained on Cap.

Right as the first two troopers reached him, Captain America whipped around and slammed them both with a flying spin kick. They fell to the ground, unconscious. Another one came at him, and Cap simply picked him up and threw him across the deck. He hit the far wall with a thud. The fourth trooper got smashed in the face by Captain America's shield.

Steve was holding his own—and then a huge pilot surprised him with a right hook. The punch sent Steve staggering backward onto one of the fighter jets. Inside, another pilot was sitting in the cockpit. He flicked a few switches and the jet burst to life. Another flick of the switch opened up the hatch, and before Steve could do anything, the pilot shot the plane forward—right into the open sky!

As the air whistled around him, Steve clung to the jet's hood. Slowly, he crept forward, making his way toward the cockpit. But the pilot wasn't about to let that happen. He executed a series of barrel rolls. Steve's legs flew out behind him as he struggled to hold on. Then the pilot pushed down the throttle and the plane nose-dived. Still, Steve hung on. When the plane righted itself, Steve pulled himself forward another few inches. He was within reach of the cockpit. But to get to the pilot, he'd have to punch out the glass. And that meant letting go with one hand. Steve took a deep breath. Before the pilot could make another move, he reached back his hand and then—*SMASH!*—he shattered the cockpit's glass, sending shards flying into the air. With one last pull, he made his way over the glass and, reaching down, released the ejector seat. Letting out a cry, the pilot was launched high into the sky.

With no one to steer it, the plane began to dive again. Climbing over the window, Captain America got into the cockpit and quickly pulled back on the throttle. When the plane was stabilized, he turned it around and flew back up, toward the Red Skull's giant plane of death: the *Valkyrie*.

During Steve's battle with the fighter jet, the Red Skull had flown the huge plane far ahead. Pressing the throttle forward as far as it could go, Steve raced after it. Blue bursts of energy fired at him from bubble turrets on top of the *Valkyrie*, but Captain America dodged them. He was closing in. When he was right at the hatch, he let up on the lever and the jet flew into the bigger plane's flight deck, landing with a flash of sparks and a shriek of brakes. Finally, it came to a stop. He had made it.

Still, the fight wasn't over. Up in the cockpit, the Red Skull was steering the plane closer and closer to the United States. And if Captain America didn't stop him, he would destroy everything and everyone Cap had been fighting for. The American Super-Soldier was battered and bruised and shaky, but he crawled out of the plane and stood up, his head held high against the evil Red Skull.

Steve had no way of knowing what was happening back at the Hydra base. He could only hope that his team, along with Peggy and Phillips, were in control and alive. He wished that he could talk to them, find out what was going on, and tell them that it would all be okay. But he couldn't. Not yet.

Right now, he was going to get into that cockpit. And then he was going to take Schmidt down. He would figure out what was in that box Schmidt held so dear and destroy it. And then he would take the plane—and all the bombs it carried—and destroy it, too.

A year ago, Steve Rogers was just an ordinary guy hoping to join the army. Now he was the courageous Captain America. People had given their lives to get him here, and he wouldn't let them down. Whatever the future held, he knew that he had to succeed. For Peggy and Bucky. For Erskine and Phillips. For the Howling Commandos. And most of all, for his country.

With heart, strength, and grim determination, Steve Rogers set off in the direction of the cockpit. It was time for the final confrontation. It was time for him to stop Johann Schmidt once and for all, no matter what the cost. It was time for the Red Skull—and all of Hydra— to learn that evil would never prevail over justice. Not while Captain America was still around to stop them.

CHAPTER 15

He found his way to the *Valkyrie*'s flight deck. There was a single pilot's chair surrounded by a half circle of instrument consoles. In the middle of the consoles was a two-handed steering yoke. Through the windows, Steve saw only open sky. Behind the pilot's chair stood a machine. Steve took a moment to look at it.

It was about four feet tall, with heavy cables coming out from it down into the floor. There was some kind of tank or chamber at the front of it, with a locking lid.

Blue light blazed inside it. Behind that was a sloping case, filled with cables and hoses. The blue glow was bright there, too, as if some kind of energy was pumping out from this machine into the rest of the plane. Maybe it powered the whole thing. Steve thought about wrecking it. That would crash the plane and save how many lives?

But he still didn't know where the Red Skull was, and Steve wanted to face him first.

Just as he thought that, he heard a sound from the back of the flight deck, where he had come in. He spun and brought his shield up just in time to absorb the blast of a Hydra energy rifle. There was the Red Skull!

Steve charged him, feeling two more energy blasts hit his shield. A third missed him and shattered one of the cockpit windows. Wind began to howl through the flight deck.

He hit the Red Skull with everything he had, using the shield like a battering ram. Schmidt reeled backward and tried to raise the rifle again. Steve smashed it with his shield. A blast of blue energy flashed out from it, blinding him. It set off sparks from other electrical equipment in the cockpit.

The Red Skull dropped the rifle and caught the shield as Steve swung it at him. He tore it from Steve's hands and smashed Steve across the face with it. Steve stumbled. He blocked Schmidt's next punch and they fought over the shield. Steve got control of it and threw Schmidt away from him. He banged into the instrument console and knocked the steering yoke hard to one side.

Both Steve and Schmidt flew into the air as the *Valkyrie* dove suddenly almost straight down. It was like there was no gravity. Steve was flung toward the back of the flight deck again, bouncing along the ceiling. The Red Skull fought the g-force of the plane's dive and reached out for a button on the instrument console. Steve couldn't get there in time to stop him. He hit the button.

The *Valkyrie* pulled out of its dive and leveled off, throwing both of them hard to the floor.

The Red Skull got to his feet first. He pulled a pistol from a holster at his belt. It looked just like a German Army Luger, but Steve could see the telltale glow of blue in its barrel. It was a Hydra energy pistol. He got the shield up and rolled away just in time as Schmidt fired several shots. They punched holes straight through the steel floor of the flight deck. "You don't give up, do you?" the Red Skull called out.

Steve faced him, crouching and ready for the Luger to fire again. "Nope," he said.

"You could have the power of the gods! Yet you wear a flag on your chest and think you fight a battle of nations!" Again Steve dodged as the Red Skull fired at him. "I have seen the future, Captain! There are no flags."

Steve had ducked behind a bulkhead at the back of the flight deck, near the door. Now he stepped out, shield ready. "Not my future," he said, and threw the shield as hard as he could.

The Red Skull tried to block the shield, but Steve had thrown it too hard. It knocked the Red Skull flat and then deflected off the wall and into the glowing blue machine behind the pilot's chair. There was an explosion that knocked them both over. Steve scrambled to pick up the shield as blue energy crackled and spat from the wreckage of the machine.

Now he could see what was inside it. There was

a cylinder holding a glowing blue cube. That was the energy source. Exposed to the open air, it was firing off strange waves of light. The air felt strange, like everything was being bent or stretched somehow. Steve looked up and couldn't believe what he saw. The roof of the *Valkyrie* wasn't there anymore. He was looking at deep space. He saw clusters of stars, brightly colored nebulas, even entire galaxies! How could that be? It was broad daylight outside.

"What have you done?" screamed the Red Skull. He pulled himself to his feet next to the broken cylinder and touched the cube. Sparks and lines of energy ran up and down his fingers. He picked the cube up and held it in the palm of his hand.

That's when things started to get really crazy.

The Red Skull stared at the cube in his hand. Steve was about to go after him again, but his eyes widened and he stayed where he was when he saw what was happening.

"No!" Schmidt howled. The light from the cube washed through his hand, and he started to disintegrate, bit by bit. He turned into streaks of light that beamed away, up into the endless space where the *Valkyrie*'s ceiling had been. Steve was amazed. It didn't look like Schmidt was in pain. He was just astonished, watching himself turn into a multicolored spray of energy. Then he was gone.

The portal closed and the view into deep space disappeared. The cube fell to the metal grating on the floor around the broken machine. It melted through the grating with a soft crackle. Then it melted through the floor below that and tumbled away out of sight.

Steve was alone in the plane, somewhere over the far north Atlantic. Maybe even over the Arctic by now. The *Valkyrie* was a very fast aircraft. He had to get control of it somehow if he could. And if he couldn't...

No matter what else happened, he had to make sure those flying bombs in the *Valkyrie*'s belly did not reach their targets.

He got into the pilot's chair and set his shield down. The steering yoke was jammed. He couldn't move the plane off its autopilot-installed bearing. There were a couple of map displays on the instrument console. One showed his current location, somewhere in the Arctic, barreling over pack ice toward North America. The other display showed a map of the area around New York City with the German caption ZIEL.

That was German for "target."

He turned on the *Valkyrie*'s radio and found the SSR frequency. "Come in," he said. "Come in, this is Captain Rogers. Can you hear me?"

When they heard Captain America's voice over the SSR control room speakers, everyone froze. Morita was the first to respond. He toggled the radio microphone and answered, "Captain Rogers, what is your position?"

Before Captain America could answer, Peggy leaned in and took the microphone away from him. "Steve, is that you? Are you all right?"

"Great," he said. "Schmidt's dead." There was a crackle of static as he spoke. Even so, everyone in the control room heard him. There were a few cheers, but not a big racket. They weren't out of the woods yet.

Peggy leaned in to find out more. "What about the plane?"

"That's a little bit tougher to explain," Captain America said after a moment.

"Give me your coordinates," Peggy said. "We'll find you a safe landing site." She looked over at the big map on the wall. The standard flight path from the Hydra base in the Alps to New York would have taken it over Great Britain and Ireland. Schmidt had probably gone farther north to avoid the potential for aerial combat. So if the plane had gone farther north, say, crossing over Iceland and Greenland, then coming back south over the remote Canadian Arctic...

There were bases. Newfoundland, Nova Scotia, Maine in the United States. There was a way to handle the problem.

On the *Valkyrie*, Steve thought about this. He wrestled with the controls and started to understand that the plane was too damaged to trust. The steering yoke barely moved to the right and left...but it did seem to go up and down. He leaned into the mike to make sure Peggy could hear him over the howl of the wind through the broken cockpit window. "This thing's moving too fast and it's headed for New York," he said. "I gotta put it in the water."

Peggy's voice crackled back at him immediately. "Please! Don't do this. We have time...."

Steve looked at the map display on the instrument console. He saw lots of ice and water. Glaciers, fjords. No cities, no towns. He figured Peggy was looking at a map, too, but she didn't know how badly the *Valkyrie* was damaged and he didn't have time to explain it to her. At his current airspeed, he was going to be within range of big cities in just a couple of minutes. "Right now I'm in the middle of nowhere. If I wait any longer, a lot of people are gonna die," he said. "Peggy, it's my choice."

It was the only choice. He opened up his compass and put it on the altimeter readout so he could look at the picture of her. Then he braced both hands on the steering yoke and pushed it forward as far as it would go.

The *Valkyrie* dove, gathering speed. The altimeter needle spun backward, faster and faster. The *Valkyrie* was dropping thousands of feet every second. Out the windows, Steve saw ice and water, still far away but getting closer fast. "Peggy," he said.

In the SSR control room, there was dead silence. Peggy swallowed and said, "I'm here."

"I'm gonna need a rain check on that dance."

She smiled a little. "All right," she said. "A week, next Saturday, at the Stork Club. Eight o'clock on the dot." She paused to gather herself and added, "Don't you dare be late. Understood?"

There was a crackle over the speakers, then Captain America's voice again. "You know I still don't know how to dance."

"I'll show you how," Peggy said. "Just be there."

"We'll have the band play something slow," Captain America said. "I'd hate to step on your—"

Static.

Steve woke up to the sound of the Dodgers on the radio. He sat up and looked around. He was in a room, maybe a hospital room? It was sunny, with a spring breeze coming in through an open window. He was wearing an SSR T-shirt, khakis, and boots. Why boots? He didn't remember putting them on. The last thing he remembered was putting the *Valkyrie* into a steep dive. He'd heard Peggy's voice over the radio and kept his eyes on her picture.

Then, nothing.

On the radio, Red Barber's voice got more excited as Pete Reiser cracked a line drive all the way to the wall. *Rizzo will score, Reiser heads to third. Durocher is going to wave him in. They look to relay, but they hold steady. Pete Reiser with an inside-the-park home run!*

But something wasn't right. He was groggy, but he could tell. Where was his shield? Where was his uniform?

A woman came into the room. Steve swung his legs over the side of the bed, still doing a mental check on himself. He seemed to be all right. He seemed to be great, in fact. It was pretty surprising. Erskine's Super-Soldier stuff was even better than Steve had thought. It had let him survive the crash of the *Valkyrie*.

"Good morning," the woman said. "Or should I say afternoon?"

Steve didn't know how to answer that. "Where am I?"

"You're in a recovery room in New York City," she said. On the radio, Red gave the score: *Dodgers take the lead. It's eight to four!*

He looked at her. She looked a little like Peggy. Steve remembered he had a date. Stork Club, eight o'clock sharp. What day was it? He hoped it wasn't Saturday yet. While he was thinking about that, something about the radio broadcast clicked. An inside-the-park grand slam? Steve remembered sitting in the grandstand at Ebbets Field as Pete Reiser headed around third for home....

Alarm bells started to go off in Steve's mind. This room was not what it seemed.

"Where am I really?" Steve asked.

"I'm afraid I don't understand," she said.

"The game," Steve said. He nodded toward the radio. "It's from May 1941. I know because I was there." He stood up and faced her. Something was wrong here and he needed to know what it was. "Now I'm going to ask you again."

"Captain Rogers—"

Steve noticed she was holding something in her hand and pressing a button on it. "Who are you?" Steve demanded. She kept pressing the button as Steve started looking for a way out.

The doors behind her burst open and soldiers came in. They weren't wearing any uniform Steve recognized. They might not be Nazis, but they sure weren't US Army, either.

He charged them and knocked them straight through the wall. It came apart more easily than it should have. Steve charged through after them. The room was a fake. It was built in the middle of a big, dark space like a warehouse. The light was strange, cold and blue. Steve looked right and left. He spotted a sign over one of the doors: EXIT.

He ran toward it and collided with another guard. Steve threw him out of the way. The guard hit the wall and went down. Steve ran on. A loudspeaker sounded an alarm. "All agents, Code Thirteen, Code Thirteen!"

Steve shoved two more guards aside. He could see another large open room ahead. There was daylight there.

When he ran into that room, he saw a row of glass doors. There were security guards charging toward him. Should he stay and fight or get outside? Instinct told him to go. He didn't have his shield and he didn't know where he was. The sooner he got away from the people chasing him, the sooner he could figure out what was going on.

Steve sprinted for the door and got outside. He knew right away he was in a city: lots of cars, tall buildings, honking horns. A split second later, he knew he was in New York when he saw street signs at the nearest corner. He was on 45th Street near Broadway. Okay, he thought. He would head for the antiques store in Brooklyn where Dr. Erskine's lab was hidden. Peggy and Colonel Phillips would be there.

Steve ran to the corner and turned down Broadway. He was so focused on getting away from the fake room and finding Peggy that at first he didn't notice how different everything was. Bit by bit it dawned on him, though. After a few seconds, it overwhelmed him. He stopped in the middle of Times Square, stunned. This was not the Times Square he remembered. There had always been billboards, throngs of tourists, people selling things from sidewalk tables...but not like this. The buildings were taller, and made of shining glass. The billboards were...they were like giant view screens, the kind of advanced gear only Hydra or the SSR had. The kind of thing Howard Stark would dream up. Pictures and words crawled across them, giant ads ten stories tall.

He spun around as something else hit him. The cars. These weren't the sleek sedans and coupes Steve remembered. They were all different shapes and sizes, all different colors. Their engines sounded different. They looked like spaceships from a movie, almost. Some of them reminded Steve of the concept flying car Howard Stark had shown at the expo. That seemed like a long time ago. *Crashing a giant airplane into the Arctic and then waking up in New York did strange things to your head,* Steve thought. How long had he been out?

Big black cars, like paddy wagons, squealed to a halt all around him, blocking traffic. Soldiers got out, wearing black uniforms Steve didn't recognize. They had eagles on their patches. From the nearest car, a bald black man with an eye patch approached Steve. He wasn't dressed like an officer, but he carried himself like one.

"At ease, soldier," he said. Steve just looked at him. There was no way to know where he was in the chain of command. Did Steve have to salute him? Was he real? What did he know about all this? "Look, I'm sorry about that little show back there," he said. "But we thought it best to break it to you slowly."

"Break what?" Steve asked.

"You've been asleep, Cap," the officer said. Steve saw sympathy on his face. "For almost seventy years."

Seventy years? He remembered the fight with Schmidt on the *Valkyrie* like it had happened just a few hours ago. The date of that operation was May 4, 1945. So now, if it was almost seventy years later, this was...

He looked again at the screens on the buildings surrounding Times Square. The date and time scrolled across the bottom of one, below some kind of news report. It was April 17, 2012.

Two thousand and twelve. Peggy would be an old, old woman now, if she was still alive. Steve sure hadn't made it to the Stork Club on time.

I crashed Hydra's superweapon and saved New York, Steve thought. *Then I woke up in the future.*

"You going to be okay?" the officer asked.

Steve thought he didn't have much choice. He had to be okay. Here he was. He was a soldier.

"Yeah," he said. "I'm just...I had a date."

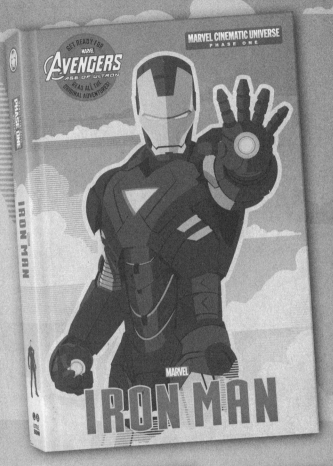